CITY OF MAGIC AND MONSTERS

A CITY OF VILLAINS NOVEL

CITY OF MAGIC AND MONSTERS

A CITY OF VILLAINS NOVEL

ESTELLE LAURE

DISNEY · HYPERION

LOS ANGELES   NEW YORK

Copyright © 2025 by Disney Enterprises, Inc.

All rights reserved. Published by Disney • Hyperion, an imprint of Buena Vista Books, Inc. No part of this book may be reproduced or transmitted in any form or by any means, electronic or mechanical, including photocopying, recording, or by any information storage and retrieval system, without written permission from the publisher. For information address Disney • Hyperion, 7 Hudson Square, New York, New York 10013.

First Edition, June 2025
10 9 8 7 6 5 4 3 2 1
FAC-004510-25086
Printed in the United States of America

This book is set in Adobe Caslon Pro/Adobe
Designed by Phil Buchanan

Library of Congress Cataloging-in-Publication Data
LCCN: 2025930589
ISBN 978-1-368-04940-5

Reinforced binding
Visit www.DisneyBooks.com

Logo Applies to Text Stock Only

To my families: the one I was born into,
the one I made, and the one I chose.
My life is rich, and I am grateful.

PART I

As everyone knows, it is because of magic's
unwieldy temperament—
its ability to appear and disappear without warning—
that it is called the great ghost.

But still . . . there are rules.

—*A People's History of the Scar*

A BRIEF TIMELINE OF MAGICAL EVENTS

The Great Death:
Thirteen years ago

The Fall:
Two years ago

The Battle of Miracle Lake:
Three weeks ago, on the anniversary
of the Great Death

The Day the World Came Apart:
Soon. Very soon.

BELLA

IT'S NEAR DARK WHEN BELLA LOYOLA BOLTS through the rain, past the abandoned, poster-glued signs declaring magic illegal, through the center of the Scar and its boarded-up storefronts. She pulls her phone from her trench coat pocket and squints through her fogged glasses, typing on the screen. A few seconds later, the gate buzzes and she bursts into the open courtyard, which is dripping with azaleas. A pink tricycle lies on its side. There are no sounds except an occasional honking and the rain as it crashes onto the cobblestone in thick curtains.

Bella tests the giant wooden security doors behind her twice, making sure they're locked, and runs toward the stairs. She could swear she's being followed even though that's impossible. The apartment building is walled in and secure. Her kitten heels clack against the stones, and her feet squelch in waterlogged leather. The book over her head is not protecting her from the rain. The weather in the Scar used to be seventy-two degrees and sunny 365 days of the year, so she sometimes forgets an umbrella, but she always remembers to pack reading material. This tome is about the power of the mind. Hers is racing.

Jasmine, who Bella hasn't been able to reach for days, alerted her to Teapot's existence; said she has a reputation for no-fuss black market deals. She needs gold to summon Mary back. So here she is.

Bella is to meet Teapot on the second floor of the walk-up apartment. She taps her coat pocket to remind herself she has a Taser in there if she really needs it. Her aunt, Stella, would cry and pray and gesticulate if she knew the risks Bella is taking. Bella cannot think about that. Her mission is too important.

Mary has been missing for nearly a month now, and Bella is tired of calling her phone and listening to her voicemail again and again. She sounds childlike and innocent on the message, but she is not. She might even be dangerous. After all, she is somewhere with James Bartholomew and Ursula and Mally Saint, and they are evil. It's not their fault. They were used and abused and tortured and given Wrong Magic, which in turn contorted them. But Mary *chose* them.

So why does Bella miss her so very much?

Why would she give her left arm for an afternoon with Mary? Mary's laugh. Mary's knowing. Mary's understanding of exactly what makes people tick. Bella is—has been—haunted by images of Mary running at her with knives, using that light of hers to melt Bella into ash.

Bella doesn't know which Mary is the real one, but whichever version she is, step one is getting her back. Bella has a strange sense that the rest of the Vanished, the children who have been disappearing from the Scar in a slow and steady drip, will follow. Bella has to take action, right action for the right side. Because Wrong Magic is not only wrong, it has the potential to annihilate everything and everyone she loves. That is why Bella will never understand magic's allure. It is at the root of everything that has gone wrong in Monarch. She herself will only use it when she has no other choice.

Which is now.

The stairwell drips with dank runoff from the rain. Bella looks like a wet possum, hair in clumps, every trace of her usual well-put-together self gone. This could be a trap. The villains can shapeshift, glamour, who knows what else. She tells herself to be brave.

Teapot descends the stairs from some upper floor. She has purple hair in a messy bun, just like Jasmine said she would, plus makeup caught in the creases of her aging skin, and snake tattoos running up her neck. Bella wishes Teapot's satin robe were cinched a little tighter.

"Let me see it," Teapot says. Bella can smell the drink on her, seeping from her pores.

"You first."

"You think I'm going to hurt you?" Teapot grins, then sucks her teeth. "I'm a businesswoman."

Teapot deals in gold, exchanges it for treasure. This Rolex is the last thing Bella is able to offer. What if the woman were to snatch it from her? Bella would have no recourse.

"Let's do it together." Bella raises her chin.

Teapot nods. Bella wraps a hand around the velvet pouch in her pocket, while the other rests on the Taser. "One, two . . ." she counts off.

"Three." A globe of gold appears in Teapot's hand, the size of a healthy radish, as Bella shows her the pouch.

Soon, gold will be harder to come by, once Legacy in the Scar figure out it's what they need to make spells work. Not the garbage Kyle and Lucas were peddling. Real magic. The good kind that grants wishes and makes dreams come true and helps people be who they want to be; the kind that lifts the heaviness of life, for a minute, an hour, long enough for suffering humans to get some relief.

Bella removes the watch from its pouch, silently thanking its donor.

After all, this belonged to his father. Teapot scans the watch and Bella can practically feel her salivating.

"Not bad," Teapot murmurs. "Pretty little trinket."

Lightning fast, Teapot snatches the watch and drops the gold into Bella's palm.

Teapot holds up the timepiece, examining the diamonds on its face, smirking. "This is worth a lot more than that," the woman says, nodding toward the gold, which Bella is sliding into the pouch. "This is a bad deal for you. Why?"

"None of your business," Bella says.

Teapot does not take offense. Instead, she shrugs. "Suit yourself. And I'm always here if you want to make another poor exchange." Teapot watches her for a moment as the rain pours all around them, then she says, almost maternally, "Stay safe out there."

When Bella reaches the ground-floor landing, she runs.

She jumps into her aunt Stella's light-blue electric car, lifting her phone so she can talk into the speaker. "Call Jasmine," she instructs as she presses the button to bring the car to life. She gets sent straight to voicemail, the same one she's been served up for the last two days.

"Hey," she says, after waiting impatiently for the beep. "I got the gold. We'll try again on the new moon. I'm coming to the paper. We need to make plans."

The windows are fogging and the thunder cracks and shakes the ground. Lightning snaps across the sky. Bella flips on the defroster and the heat, and zips toward the *Genie's Lamp*, Jasmine's newspaper, warming her free hand by the vent. She touches the pouch to make sure it's still there, that the gold is safe, and she's going to have the chance to get the summoning spell right this time.

As she goes left on Desire Avenue she passes the Layer Cake and the

Wand Emporium, both shuttered, and she tears open a peanut butter chocolate protein bar, her first sustenance of the day. Her nervous system is a mess, but breathing will have to wait. She chews as she passes posters of the Red Queen, Maleficent, the sea witch, Captain Hook, and the Mad Hatter that are plastered over every surface in this part of town, except where the buildings have been torn down.

Yellow construction equipment sits abandoned in the rain, but as soon as it lets up the workers will be back, ripping up the neighborhood, making room for Uptown Coffee Company and the Noodle Spoon and all the other franchises invading, tearing away at four hundred years of history. Bella's cheeks heat, and she tries to focus on the road as she turns into the warehouse district. Mally Saint's father, Jack Saint, and Ursula both once lived in this neighborhood, but Ursula is gone and Jack has moved to a mansion on the outskirts of town. Crows no longer circle the air above their apartment building. Everything is changing.

Bella slides up to the *Genie's Lamp*, the gold ball safely in her pocket. She turns on her hazard lights, jumps out of the car, and peers through the window. The lights are off. Where journalists can usually be seen puttering around, drinking coffee and writing on whiteboards, leaning over their desks, it's now as dead as dried mud. Something flaps in the wind and Bella goes to the door, reads the sign:

CLOSED UNTIL FURTHER NOTICE BY ORDER OF THE WATCH.

Bile rises, a warning in the back of her throat.

Great ghost, what is happening?

What is happening to the Scar?

She has to make sure Jasmine is okay. Knowing how dedicated Jasmine is to the paper, Bella can only imagine how upset she must be. She gets back in the car, jams on the accelerator, and flies down empty streets toward Jasmine's apartment. She tells herself to slow down, that she's going to have an accident. She hums a tune to comfort herself, something calming, reassuring, but it's no good. She pulls into the parking lot at Jasmine's building. There's no security, so she goes straight up the stairs three floors, then runs down the hallway until she gets to the door. She knocks once, twice. And again.

She knows as soon as she sees the expression on Jasmine's fiancé Al's face that something terrible has happened. Al is always a little wild, but in a journalist way. Sometimes his clothes are a bit rumpled. Sometimes he eats dinner at his desk, and on occasion he seems far away and she can tell he's thinking.

This is different. This is more than a shut-down newspaper.

Dark circles form half-moons under his eyes, and his white T-shirt is dingy. His jeans hang off his hips, loose from days of wear. Bella is gifted at picking up clues. These are bad.

"I was going to call you." He runs his fingers through his black hair.

"Is Jasmine here?" Bella says, eyes flickering around the space behind him.

"No, she—" Al's phone rings, and he presses the button to answer it and tucks it against his ear. "Yeah?" he says. He shakes his head and puts up one finger, inviting Bella to come in but not to talk. "Yes . . . yes. . . . No, she was meeting a source. . . . Friday . . . I know. . . . Well, if you hear anything, let me know. . . . No, I have a few more places to try. . . . Hang on, I need to grab a pen."

Reality knocks Bella sideways. Another friend is gone.

Maybe the world really is at its end. Maybe too much damage has been done. If people can just disappear en masse and no one does anything, what does that say about the fabric of reality?

Al wanders around the corner, still on the phone, as warm, furry fingers entwine with Bella's. It's Abu, Al's monkey. He looks at her kindly with worried brown eyes, and she lets him guide her to the kitchen. The apartment is usually pristine, decorated with flowers and pops of blue, mosaics and peacocks displayed throughout. Now Jasmine's table is littered with empty food containers, and Al's notes are all over, scrawled on receipts, on random pieces of paper. Bella scans them quickly. Hospitals, mostly. Names of people she doesn't know: Harold Dixon, Donna D'Amico, and so on. They are all crossed out. And in a plastic baggie, Jasmine's cell phone. She recognizes the worn blue butterfly sticker on the back. She feels sick, like maybe she needs to vomit.

Al's not going to find Jasmine at any hospitals. If Jasmine is gone like the rest of them, she's somewhere only magic can reach. Chief Charlene Ito hasn't been seen since Jasmine's article, which pointed to her part in creating the villains. She's not at all sure that the Monarch police are on the up-and-up, even with Chief Ito gone.

But it's like people have blinders on, like they don't want to hear it, don't want to acknowledge that change has come to their door and there is no putting the genie back in the lamp.

Al's leaning against the wall, scribbling on yet another scrap of paper.

"Have you eaten, Abu? Are you hungry?" she whispers to the monkey, trying to distract herself.

He signs no, then pats her hand and points to a picture of Jasmine on a nearby credenza. Jasmine loves to traipse around the city looking for hidden treasures, and this piece was one of her biggest scores. She talked that poor antique dealer down until he was practically crying. That's Bella's favorite thing about Jasmine. She is relentless. Bella doesn't want to picture her suffering, yet that is the image that comes to mind. Some sick, toxic, magical dungeon.

Abu makes a sad, keening noise.

"I know . . ." Bella says.

Abu shrugs, looking mournful, as Al sits down at the table, finally off the phone. "Jasmine . . . she hasn't been here since Friday night."

It's Sunday. That's two days. Too long.

"She went to meet a source and never came back." He puts up a hand. "And before you ask, I don't know who or why. She said she would tell me everything after. I'm so stupid. I thought she would be fine because she always shares her location with me and . . . well . . . because she's Jasmine." He rests his forehead in his palms, elbows leaned on the table. "She's invincible, you know? Or she's supposed to be. But then when she didn't come back, I traced her cell to a warehouse a couple blocks over. Abu found it on the ground, just lying there."

Abu whimpers.

"That means she was taken by force, because you know J and her phone," he says, raising his head, an affectionate tilt to his mouth creeping through the worry and exhaustion before dropping off again. "But I've called every hospital, every shelter, every hotel and motel, just in case, to cover my bases. I can't just sit here."

Bella thinks of Jasmine and her ticking, tapping, perfectly manicured fingernails, typing away, doing so many important things. She wills herself with the full force of her spirit not to dissolve into hysteria. There is work to be done, and she needs to heed her own advice: Bella has been telling Mary Elizabeth since day one that she is too driven by emotion, and that is dangerous. Bella's got to prove she is logical and can think straight under pressure. But she has known Jasmine since college, when they went through the criminal justice program together. They were babies when they started, but emerged women. If Mary Elizabeth has a hold on Bella's heart, Jasmine has her spirit, fiery and bold.

"I'm trying to get anyone in law enforcement to take it seriously," Al says, still grasping the phone, "but the cops keep telling me she probably went on vacation or something. Nobody cares about us. Plus . . . you know Jas made some enemies in the government."

Jasmine is in the business of irritating the gentry, reporting on the rich and corrupt. She's so careful, so responsible, so street smart. She must have let down her guard. Bella wishes she had been there. She can tell Al feels the same.

"Okay, well, we can't give up, obviously. And if the police aren't listening, we'll have to deal with it ourselves. We have to start somewhere," Bella says, gathering her energy.

"Yeah?" Al says.

And now she says the thing that she hasn't yet spoken out loud, the thing she knows might send Al into even more of a panic. "Have you thought about the Vanished? I mean—"

"Why?" He cuts her off. "Do you think she's one of them?"

"I don't know," Bella says, as gently as she can. None of them have been located, dead or alive. "It's a possibility."

"She's a little too old to fit the demographic, don't you think? It's kids, twelve to sixteen."

Al's strapping, with dark skin and broad shoulders, but right now he looks small, pale, even.

"It *is* kids," Bella says, "but we don't know why they're gone, or where they've gone." She pats him on the shoulder. She's not a hugger. "It's as good a place as any to start."

He lets out a sigh that turns into a single sob. Abu clambers onto his shoulder, and Al gives him a squeeze.

CITY OF MAGIC AND MONSTERS

"We will find her," Bella says, testing the words in her mouth for truth. "We will find her and she will be fine and we will go on."

Abu leaps into Bella's lap and rests his head against her chest. She strokes his fur and thinks. There are theories about where all those kids have gone: human trafficking, death cults . . . But Bella knows it has to have something to do with the return of magic. It's an Occam's razor type of deduction. The kids went missing just after magic came back, after the villains disappeared to parts unknown. That is the most logical assumption, besides which, when people disappear without magic, they have to be somewhere. These ones are *nowhere*. All those broken mothers and fathers and aunts and uncles, all those weeping grandparents.

Once, before the Great Death, when magic left the world, House Fantasia, where Bella was raised, was a place where wishes came true, and when the children began to Vanish, their caregivers took up residence in front of Bella's home, thinking . . . hoping . . . that if magic was back at all, House Fantasia would be able to grant their wishes and bring home the kids.

But House Fantasia couldn't do anything at all. Because magic was only back for the villains.

And now Jasmine is nowhere, too.

Out the window, past the rain, across the street of honking cars, Bella spies another of the posters warning the Scar's population about the villains and the Red Queen. SHE IS EVERYWHERE, it reads. Bella shudders, thinking of the mysterious woman in red who was slinking through the streets, slipping through security, breaking monsters like the Mad Hatter out of prison.

"You field calls. See if she's anywhere we might have missed. Shelters, with relatives . . . anything. I'll update you," Bella says, thinking again of the gold in her pocket. "I don't know where they all are," she says, "but I am damn well going to find them. I will bring Jasmine home to you." She pauses. "I will."

She dips back into the rain, hoping she hasn't just told the biggest lie of her life.

ONE

We do not choose where magic takes root. Where there is a Seed mark, there lies potential, but only magic decides how to evolve.

—*The People's History of Magic*

WE CALL IT NEVERLAND, AND IT IS BEAUTIFUL.

I'm up on the mast of the *Mary Elizabeth*, inching along with new muscles, pulling myself up into the basket for a better view. My legs are sore from combat practice today and I can feel a new layer of peeling skin on my nose from my hours on deck, fighting in the sun. Every muscle hurts, and gods, I love it. A meal of roasted quail and lollyblossom cupcakes, along with fresh yeast rolls and summer salad, is coming, to be served at the captain's table, but I want just a few more moments of peace.

I wave to Mally and James, who are resting on deck chairs with peppermint-swirl covers. James's dog, Barnacle, is nearby, his brown paws sticking straight up, and Hellion, Mally's crow, stands at attention on the back of Mally's chair. When James waves back, I take a long look at my surroundings. We used to have a whole fleet of ships, but the chief and I did some redecorating, made the *Legacy* and the *Loyalty* bigger and better. They house the Vanished now, and the two ships flank the main ship. Ursula backstrokes between the ships. Peering out over endless water in all directions gives me a happy vertigo.

The chief says to enjoy these quieter days, because they won't be here long. I've been a city girl my whole life, surrounded by gray, by skyscrapers, by wishes for what came before the Great Death, when magic abandoned us. I never imagined I would be here. Yes, I had to leave Aunt Gia behind. And Bella. But someday soon, they'll understand why. I resist visions of their disappointed faces and let the breeze blow away my worries, then search for signs of storms, of other boats, of anything unexpected coming our way, but everything looks good. It's still us, only us, as it has been for all the weeks since my arrival here, in between dimensions, deep in the waters of Miracle Lake, in a world we invented. We all left people behind—James left his fairy godmother, Della, Ursula left her mother and sister, Mally left her dad. And the chief? Well . . . she left everything.

"All okay up there, toots?" Urs calls, pausing to tread water, her tentacles rolling around her. She caught me thinking.

"Clear skies ahead!" I give her a thumbs-up and she smiles and hums, hums and smiles, then resumes her languid circles.

"Hey, come down!" James calls, a hand over his brow. Barnacle doesn't get up but twists his head toward us with interest. "I've been apart from you long enough. Can't take another second." He's gone a deep brown under the blazing sun, and his hair is longer and wavier than it used to be. He's in his usual T-shirt and linen pants, hook glinting, and I find him altogether pleasing.

I take one last look at the ship's reflection in the water and shimmy down, careful not to get splinters. I land with a thump and James scoops me up in his arms, lifts me off my feet, and plants a kiss on my waiting lips.

"Hi," I say, then peer around him. "Where'd Mally go?"

"She said she needed some time alone." He looks toward the stairs that lead down to each of our rooms, which are next to Mally's.

"Time alone she decided on when you called for me, because she's secretly in love with you?" I tease.

James grins, bolstered by the idea of us fighting over him, which neither of us would ever do. "No," he says, wiping the glee off his face with some difficulty. "Something else. Something's going on with her, and she won't tell me what it is. But she's been acting funny."

"Mally . . . funny?" I shrug. "Hmmm. I've never thought of that as one of her attributes."

"Don't be jealous," he says, nuzzling my neck.

"I told you when I got here that I don't care if she has a crush on you as long as we both know you're mine."

"Always yours," he says, kissing my forehead with warm lips. He leans into me, smelling of salt and the sulfuric afterburn of magic.

"You were brewing?" I ask.

"Had to make a new batch for tomorrow when we go to the Scar, and you know . . . we don't have magic to pluck from the sky there. Not yet." He pulls me into him by the base of my spine, and we kiss. We still need infusions of magic when we leave here, but someday we won't. That's the whole point.

"Wait, wait," I say, pulling away. "Give me a second." I sweep my hands over my body and give myself a quick magical glamour scrub down. I sprinkle my skin with the smell of warm vanilla and change from my black shorts and white T-shirt into red pants and my combat

CITY OF MAGIC AND MONSTERS

boots, along with a black corset top. I smooth out my hair and curl it into beach waves. I mint my breath and, as I flick my hand in front of my face, I think neutral makeup and deep crimson lips. I feel the Red Queen—who was once an alien, ominous presence—peaceful and quiet inside me now that I'm not trying to exorcize her. She beats under my footsteps, as much a part of me as my shadow, and she makes me whole.

"Nice," James murmurs. "But I like you dirty, too." His fingers spark, and he presents me with a glittering black dahlia. I take it and lean into his neck, letting the flower fall to my side. Magic is not our only currency.

He kisses me again, soft lips pressing against mine, before letting his hook rest against my waist. As soon as we've parted, I crave him. It doesn't matter how many years go by or how much happens between us, it's always the same.

"Get a room!" Urs yells. She slurps over the edge, dripping with ocean water as she clambers onto the deck.

"You get a room," James says, laughing between kisses. "And mind your own business."

"Your business is my business, sweetie," Urs calls as she scoots past us and down the stairs, presumably to get ready for dinner. "Sorry to break it to you!"

"Well, hello, you two." Ito comes through the main doors and I feel how I always do when I see her, like I'm backstage at the most important play ever. Like I am this person and also the little girl whose family's murder was solved by her. To me, she is half goddess, half human, all witch, and that's my favorite combination.

"Hi, Chief," James says, straightening his clothes, cheeks reddening.

"I thought I'd come up here myself and tell you dinner's almost ready." She looks summery in her white silk blouse and baggy pants, a delicate slice of a gold crown resting on her head, breezier than I ever thought was possible when I knew her as Monarch's chief of police. She was uptight and cold, all business, always in a suit. Here, she's different. I thought she might be a monster. I had it all wrong.

"Mary, if you don't mind, I'll have you on my right tonight," she says.

"Of course." That means a personal conversation. I swell with pride, even as James puffs up his chest behind Ito and makes an *ooh-la-la* face at me.

"James, would you gather everyone?" Ito says, almost catching him acting a fool. "It's been a long day, and I suspect they're ready to eat."

"Aye, aye." He whistles for Barnacle, who leaps to attention, and the two of them disappear from view.

I follow Ito to the long captain's table, away from the prying eyes and ears of the crew, who are busily milling about. The evening air crackles and hums with magic, and it is as delicious as the food is sure to be, like fluffy angel wing cake. The sky has darkened above us and swirls with unfamiliar stars, a nowhere galaxy of nothing planets in a place that doesn't exist.

"Dinner is served!" Smee shouts as we sit. The Lost Boys tromp in with much fanfare. Wibbles plays the kazoo. Damien bangs on a drum. The rest float silver platters behind them. Ursula shows up with her human legs instead of her tentacles, her shell necklace resting in the hollow of her throat, and joins us at the table. Caleb Rothco, the Mad Hatter, slides into his seat, hardly paying any attention to anyone, muttering to himself, his meat cleavers glinting from the holster on his chest. Mally finds her place as Hellion flies off and perches on the boat's rail, waiting for the meat she always feeds him when she's finished with her plate.

"Wonderful," Ito proclaims, clapping in time with the drum until all the food is on the table. "Feast!" she says with a flourish, and we all dig in.

You would think we hadn't eaten in days. It's the long hours of physical training and the weeks of brewing magic. They quicken the appetite and make us yearn for sweetness and salt. I sink my teeth into a yeast roll. The food here is the best I've ever had, elevated by that extra thing we can't name. And that's saying something, because the food in the Scar is amazing.

"I wanted to talk to you," Ito says, when I've ripped my quail to pieces and sucked the juice from its cracked bones. She accepts a mineral water from Nibs, as tall and narrow as he is thin. "Tomorrow you'll be going into Monarch to fetch the last addition to the Vanished."

"I thought we were done bringing on new people," I begin. "We're so far into the training—"

"Yes. I've made an exception. An agreement, if you will." She glances toward Ursula, who raises her glass to the chief.

"Morgie," I guess out loud.

"Correct," the chief says. "More family. What could be better?"

I imagine Morgie at this table, with us, demanding more rolls, more attention, more more more. I used to love Ursula's little sister. I don't know anymore. But I understand why she needs to be here. I've heard her pleas to join us coming through Ito's mirror. I used to do the same thing, beg and beg to be with my friends instead of trapped in the nightmare the Scar had become. I know the pain of being left behind, and Morgie craves magic just like the rest of us.

"She'll be in school when you get her, and we want to make a splash, a scene," the chief goes on. "The plan is for you and Ursula and James to unleash magic, to let the Scar know we still have it, that the Battle at Miracle Lake was not a fluke. And we want to scare the devil out of the

Narrows kids while we're at it. They'll be nervous when they see what we can do. And they should be."

I lean back from my plate. This is a complete departure from our prior instructions. Our whole mission has been to remain ghostlike and invisible and snatch the kids who want to join us in the dead of night. The chief sends us through her magic mirror, and we are in and out of the Scar in under a minute.

Going to Monarch High?

That's a whole other thing.

There will be security, Principal Iago (who hates me), hostile Narrows, and who knows what else.

"I can see you have qualms, Mary, and that's perfectly natural," she says. "But the time has come to leave the shadows behind, to claim who you are." She takes a sip of her water. I still haven't seen her take a bite of food. "In front of everyone," she adds as an afterthought.

She doesn't say it, but I know she means my aunt Gia. Gia, who raised me, loved me, supported me. Gia, who has no idea where I am. Or who I am. Not anymore. Fully revealing myself to her is no small ask.

"But that's not the main thing," she says, covering my hand with hers. "I'd like you to portal tomorrow."

"Me?" My stomach gurgles uncomfortably. During the Battle at Miracle Lake, when I rescued James and Mally and Ursula from the labs where they were being experimented on, I made glass disappear just by thinking about it.

I opened a portal in the wall.

I cut off James's hand to save him.

But all of that was desperate. I wasn't thinking. I was only reacting. As I turn my attention back to Ito, the magical energies around us intensify, swirling and dancing, like the air itself can hear us and is urging us along, whispering that I can do it. But what if I can't? I feel the familiar zing of purpose, the lurch of attachment to the chief, and a pride I never had before she took me on and let me join her here.

Ito's expression darkens, a storm of concern flickering. "I have one more thing I need to talk to you about." She pauses, and I can tell she's thinking over her choice of words. "I know you love Bella Loyola."

My stomach tightens. There has long been an issue between Bella and the chief, and when I first got here the chief was clear it was Bella or them. We've built trust these last weeks, trust that is important to me now.

"I know you want her to understand you and to join our side," the chief goes on. "But Bella's desires run deep, Mary. It's far worse than you think. She craves not just power but dominion over all magic itself. Her ambitions have led her down a treacherous path. She thinks she understands, but she doesn't. She thinks she knows the right way, but she has no idea. She thinks I'm the one she's trying to fight, but I'm not." She takes a breath. "My informants tell me she's got gold now, and you know gold and Legacy blood along with Miracle Lake water make magic when there is none. Soon enough, she'll find us. And we have to be ready before that happens. We need to move quickly." She considers me for a moment. I straighten my back. We both know I have only ever been able to portal in moments of desperation, fits of anger, and intense fear. "When we go through to the Scar, we will need to be in three places at once: at city hall, on Desire Avenue, and at Miracle Lake," she says. "I can open the portals, but I will need you to hold them, to keep them steady."

The weight of her words settles into my cells, leaving invisible imprints on my skin. "I will try."

"You done down there?" James calls from his end of the table, where he is clearly feeling bored and left out.

The chief leans back, taking her glass of bubbly water with her. "I think we are."

"Woohoo!" James caws. "Time for me and my girl is afoot." He slaps a hand on the table and grins at me. "Get your dessert to go. A warm night calls for gawping at the moon and dancing."

"Yes, Captain," I tease as he impales a pink-frosted cupcake on the end of his hook and gives it a lick.

"Young love," the chief says. "Warms my heart." She bends across the table to whisper, "Have your fun, and then . . . think about what I said." She exclaims with pleasure when she finally begins to eat. "So good!"

And in that moment, as the stars above shimmer and the ocean laps against the ships, I feel a bond to the chief.

We'll see what tomorrow brings.

I hope I'm worthy of the faith she has in me.

It feels like everything depends on it.

TWO

Before the Scar was inhabited by people, a pocket of
magic waited beneath the ground, untapped.

—A People's History of the Scar

IF WE WEREN'T IN THE MIDDLE OF A REVOLUTION,
it would be the perfect summer day, one for lying in the grass,
cloud making, kissing, and drinking gooseberry-lemonade slush-
ies. I try to conjure the smell of the Scar, the shops selling records
and fake glass slippers and the best, tiniest baked goods. It used to
be vibrant, colorful, music on every corner, art on every building.
Even without magic, the Scar was enchanting. Sneaking around
the way we "villains" do when we cross through the mirror back
home, we never get to see the outside, and just like the feeling of
being with my parents and playing with my sister, Mira, the memories are fading.

Since James, Ursula, and I will be fetching Morgie, the Vanished
have a day off. Smee and the Lost Boys are looking after them, and
the Vanished are taking full advantage, already playing pickleball,
backgammon, and bocce, or reading, fighting each other in video

games, and jumping in and out of the huge on-deck pool the chief and I magicked when we updated the main ship. Some of them are even lying out in bikinis, soaking up the sun, drinking cold, sweet beverages laced with fruit and salt. They watch as I pass them, like I'm someone important and frightening.

I join Ursula at the side of the boat where she's staring at the water, deep down to places only she has been, where she seems to be more and more these days. I want to ask her what she's thinking, but I know if I do, she'll answer with a joke. The truth is hidden within her, murky as a seaweed forest.

"Heya," I say.

"Heya," Urs answers, giving me a sidelong glance, before she does a double take. "Wowee." She whistles and waggles her eyebrows at me and my crimson sheath dress.

"Thanks, friend," I say. "Trying to be prepared for the cameras."

"Cameras?" She nods. "Ohhh, I get it. You mean when we go to the school. Is that what the chiefy wanted last night? All that whispering?"

I shrug. "I guess. She wants us to make a splash today."

"My specialty." Urs squints like she's trying to see me better. "And?" she asks. "What else did she say?"

I hesitate but then say, "She told me Bella's been causing trouble."

"Oh sure." Urs nods. "Never liked that Goody Two-shoes."

I think back to what the chief said last night about Bella's ambitions. About her wanting magic for herself. A vision of a power-hungry Bella tries to rise up, but my brain immediately rejects it. That's just not her. I respect the chief, but she's off the mark when it comes to Bella. "I know she annoys you," I say, "but she was my friend, and a good one. She doesn't know any better. She's doing what she thinks is right, and who can blame her? Our pictures are all over the Scar like we're ogres."

CITY OF MAGIC AND MONSTERS

"Being against us is so boring, though. She'd have a lot more fun if she'd loosen up."

"Mhmm," I say. I don't like to talk about Bella. Not with Urs. "So . . . you think Morgie will like it here?"

She turns around to lean her elbows against the railing, her giant gold hoops pressing into her shoulders. "Who knows? She's a pain in every single one of my tentacles, that kid. I don't know what I'm going to do with her. Teach her some lessons, that's the only thing that's for sure."

Bringing Ursula's little sister here means leaving their mother without either of her daughters. No one to look out for her. Plus, Morgie is a handful. Last time I saw her at Monarch High, she was awful, demanding magic, threatening me with her ridiculous high school "alpha" status, and totally throwing accusations at Ursula. Hopefully we'll be able to end this soon, and Ursula and Morgie will get to go back to their mother. Then *all* the Vanished can go home.

But first, we turn city hall into rubble.

"Morgie thinks I did this on purpose," Ursula goes on. "That I left her behind or something."

The water is different here than in other oceans. It's still, but it isn't light blue or green. We can't see ocean life swimming under the surface. There's no hint of how far above the bottom we are. We can only see our own little faces and the ship—its red flag with the black heart at its center—as clearly as a reflection in a mirror.

"I'm so glad we're here together," I say. "Seriously." We used to run through the streets of the Scar and dip in and out of shops, thrift, ingratiate ourselves to merchants who ran bodegas, and hang out in the school playground to swing on rusty equipment and talk long past curfew. Ursula was always betting on something, and it meant everything to me that I could be a part of that. Because before I met her, I had no one.

No one but my family. And then they were gone.

"Aw, you're the sweetest," she says. "I'm glad, too."

If it weren't for the grayish tinge to her skin, I could believe it was the before times, when we used to get dressed up and go to school, worry about tests and homework and whatever new movie was coming out that Friday. She still has that red mouth, clumpy black lashes, hair so blond it's white, up in two space buns. She almost looks the same.

But everything is different now.

She kisses me on the cheek, and her lips are as cold as a cadaver's.

We meet in Chief Ito's quarters, spacious rooms with a desk, a big table surrounded by chairs, bookshelves lining the walls. The cauldron that sits in the corner underneath her collection of bottles and oils and herbs reeks of rosemary and mushrooms, plus something else, a rotting sweetness. A luxurious bed draped in white is visible in the attached bedroom. Everything else is black leather. A skull trapped and hanging in a bell jar stares down at us. And most importantly, the chief's mirror sits in the center of the table. It's no bigger than a grocery-store paperback book, rectangular, silver with a plain black border. It looks like a mirror you could buy in any big-box store in any country, and yet it's the only way off this ship.

The chief rests a hand on my shoulder and I turn my attention to her. "I'm proud of you. This is going to go fine, don't worry. You were made for this."

"Yeah, if you screw it up, we'll be cosmic goo in some parallel universe," Urs says, grinning. "No presh."

CITY OF MAGIC AND MONSTERS

"That's not going to happen," the chief says, giving Ursula a harsh glare. "You've portaled accidentally without issue, and your weeks here have made you strong. Remember, this place has fortified you as surely as the drills we've been doing with the Vanished have helped their muscles grow. You're so much stronger than you were when you arrived. You'll do an excellent job and have everyone back here safe and sound in no time."

"Yes, ma'am," I say.

"And you two." Ito rakes her attention around the circle, resting her eyes first on James, then on Urs. "Magic away. Make it a day to remember. We want phones out and impact made. We want the Narrows to know who we are and what we're capable of. We want them quaking in their driving moccasins, understand?"

"Yes, Chief," we all say.

"Don't hold back," she says. "Let them know they can make magic illegal and threaten us as much as they want. We won't be playing by those rules." Her words shift the energy in the room, electrifying everything. I tighten my jaw, braced for what's about to happen.

"You ready?" James checks his pocket watch, which used to belong to my grandfather. "We want to make it before third period ends."

The chief stands back, giving us access to the mirror. "Go, my ducklings. Do good work."

A deep quiet comes over the room. I'm aware the chief is watching me, and I want to perform the way she wants me to. I focus, think about my destination, that we want to go to the Scar, to Monarch High, to Morgie's math class. I will us to break into Monarch, the three of us together. There's a shimmer in the mirror, and for a second I think I've been successful. Our reflections waver and wobble, but then the mirror goes flat, dead, and inanimate. I try again, but it's even worse this time.

30

Nothing happens, not even a glimmer of a flint to spark the magic in me.

"I can't do it," I say, softly. "I'm sorry, Chief."

"We need to hurry," James says. "Timing is everything. Mary, you can practice later."

I meet the chief's eyes. She gives me a reassuring nod, faces the mirror, and raises her arms to the heavens. "Mirror, mirror, on the wall, take my children to the high school hall."

I'm preoccupied, even as the mirror begins to shake and clatter jumpily across the table. I've failed again.

"Stop," James whispers. "You're spiraling, and we've got other things to worry about now. You will get this. Later."

The mirror bucks and widens, popping off the table, onto the floor, until it grows into a portal big enough to fit a human body, and bigger. My throat tightens with humiliation, but I try to focus on what's in front of me.

"Here we go, babycakes," Urs says, letting out a loud, joyful cackle.

The ground melts.

"Now," the chief says.

Ursula bumps her butt into mine. Then she jumps, hooting and whooping as she goes.

James and I hold hands and leap. We tumble and roll. I am half here and half in the Scar. I am widened, stretched, all intention and motion, muscle and sinew and hope.

Now we are somewhere and nowhere. Not on the ship, and not yet in the Scar. In a glass window and outside of it. Our feet are held in midair as if by some invisible force. We are two stories up and floating outside Morgie's classroom. James grins at me, and his teeth look like a monster's.

CITY OF MAGIC AND MONSTERS

We peer inside. Ms. Aldana—small, wiry, with long braided black hair—is writing on the whiteboard.

I wasn't expecting it to be her.

She used to work with me on geometry, back when I was a normal tenth grader with braces. Such a long time ago.

And the freshmen. They are all in gray cotton tops, with gray bottoms to match.

Monarch High is as familiar to me as my own skin. The halls. The espresso cart. The bathrooms with their sparkly white tiles and tagged-up walls. I can picture it all, even from here. But the kids are drab, slouched in their seats in uniform, and that is new. I can't even tell the difference between a Legacy student and a Narrows kid, which I suppose is the point.

James raises his hook and motions forward.

The glass, still under our command, dematerializes.

We land, feet on the ground, in the classroom, and the glass seals behind us.

"Urs!" Morgie squeals. She flings herself out of her desk and into Ursula's arms, then into mine with such velocity she almost knocks me over. "Mary!" Her lips are painted a bright, dangerous purple.

Ms. Aldana stops her lesson, mid calculation. Her face goes rigid. The color leaves her cheeks. I try to imagine what we must look like to her. This probably isn't what she meant when she told me to stop by her classroom whenever I felt like it.

"Hi, sweetums," Urs says to Morgie. "What happened to everyone? Did the color coppers attack the school and drain out all the fun? You look like worms!"

"This is the new school uniform." Morgie tugs at her bland shirt. "Can you believe it?"

32

"I can believe it," Urs says, "but I'm not going to stand for it."

"Are you taking me to magic?" Morgie squees. "I'm going to lose it if I don't get out."

"Sure am," Urs says, "but first, I've got work to do!"

"Hello, everyone!" James adds. "Why so glum?"

"They're in school, silly, bored to death." Urs swings her hips from side to side. "Whaddya say we liven up the place?"

The kids are still, all staring at us with unfocused eyes and dead spirits.

"Children." Ms. Aldana's voice is measured and careful, like she's scared if she talks too loudly, we'll start murdering her students. "Don't move. Don't speak. Think of your families and stay where you are."

"You don't have to be afraid of us," I say, trying to meet her eyes, to show her my kindness. "We're not going to hurt anyone. We just want Morgie. She belongs with us. And we've never taken anyone who didn't want to come."

"Don't bother," James says, his face in the shadowed corner behind me. "No one absurd enough to believe we would ever hurt one of our own is going to listen."

"We're good," I say to Ms. Aldana, not able to help myself. "We have always been good."

"Enough of that." Ursula swishes down the aisle. "Let's get this party started!" She waves her hands over the class. I give up on Ms. Aldana and join Ursula. I start by bringing a cell phone to life, which blasts loud music.

"Nice," Urs says as she transforms one girl's makeup from drab to glam. All around us, gray turns to greens and blues and reds and yellows, as we splash the classroom with brightness. Sequins and feathers appear around necks. Studded belts and fishnet stockings spruce up those sad outfits.

The kids come to, as though waking from a long dream. They start to make noise, like they should, gasping and laughing at the sweet, delicious magic all around them.

As Urs circles the room, I stir the air. I dance papers off desks. Books off shelves. I animate whiteboard markers to scrawl a giant happy face and a vase of beautiful flowers. I may have failed at getting us here, but now the magic is billowing through me, sparking all over the place.

I'm having a great time, the *best* time, when a flamingo flaps through the window, lands on Ms. Aldana's desk, and looks around, confused. I don't know where the bird came from, but Urs and I dissolve into laughter.

Ms. Aldana is yelling now, trying to see past the bird. "Kidnapping! Theft! Murder?" Her voice rises above the fray. Phones are out everywhere. All of this is being captured. It's exactly what the chief wanted. "That is not *good*!" Ms. Aldana cries.

"We want to come, too!" the kids say. They grab for Ursula's arms, but she glides between them, out of reach. "Take us!"

Finally, Ursula is done. I wave a hand, and all the objects go still. The markers fall from the board, the books climb back onto the shelves, the air softens.

"Awwwww," the kids complain in unison. All the phones are trained on us. Now's the time for us to say what we need to say.

"The Vanished we take want to go," I say. "They're being saved, not stolen."

A somber-looking girl who is now in a fruit-print dress holding a lemon-shaped bag says, "Are you taking all of us, then? Are we all going to be Vanished?"

"No," I say. "Not today."

Groans and protests grow around us. But we've won the room. They don't want to do math. They want to come with us. They're all leaning in toward us, all riveted. Not afraid. Not anymore.

"Come on," James says to Urs and Morgie. "Time to go." Then to the kids in the class. "Magic is your birthright. Color, individuality, courage . . . don't let them take it from you. Watch this space for more!"

"Legacy Loyalty," a girl with curtain bangs and bright blue eyes says. A chorus rises behind her.

"Legacy Loyalty! Legacy Loyalty! Legacy Loyalty!"

Guards burst through the door.

"Oh no." I turn to face the windows again. "Chief, bring us back!"

Nothing happens. The glass is thick and strong. I give James a worried look.

"Come on, Chiefypoo," Urs whispers through clenched teeth. "Bad time for us to be trapped."

"Hold it right there," one of the guards says and we all turn around with our hands up. The two men are winded and pasty like they've been running down the halls since we got here. They're a far cry from the Watch. Those lackeys had gray uniforms and slick new SUVs and weapons, and there's no sign of them.

"If you don't get out of here right now, I'm going to turn you into worms—actual real worms," Urs says. "Then, when you're shrunken down and helpless, I'm going to take you home and put you in a pail and bury you in dirt, where you will grow the Red Queen's favorite rosebush, and no one will ever find you, and you will never, ever go home again. Is that what you want?"

The two men, who don't look much older than us, exchange looks, like they're trying to decide what to do next.

"She's a total loose cannon." I make a little worm motion with my index finger and scrunch up my face. "And I do love my roses."

"What do you make an hour? Minimum wage?" Urs says to them. "Nothing wrong with that. It's an honest paycheck. But ask yourselves, is it worth it?"

For a second I think they're going to slink away, but then I see them tense. "We've got orders," the smaller one says.

Ursula swishes toward them.

The little one pulls a Taser from his pocket and brandishes it at us.

"You kiddin' me?" Ursula says, pausing midstep.

I look at James, and he shrugs.

"Get 'em!" Morgie cries, jumping behind Urs as the smaller guard lunges toward us, pressing the button on his Taser.

Before the Taser darts hit her, Ursula hurls magic from her palms. Flashes of blue careen across the room, slap into the men, and to my relief, instead of being killed the guards turn into worms, as promised, wriggling on the floor.

Cries of fear and surprise are growing wildly all around us. The kids are scared, and that's not what we want.

"Come on, Mary," Urs yells as a new batch of men appear in the doorway and sprint toward us. I guess the Watch is still around after all.

"Freeze," James calls out, holding up his watch. The whole room pauses. James stopping time is a brief trick, but hopefully his magic will last long enough that we can get out of here.

The guards have gone completely still except for their eyeballs, which twitch and roll in their sockets. Everyone in the classroom is in suspended animation, as Ursula strikes again. The Watch guards shrivel and join the other two on the floor.

Just when I think we might make it out of this place without killing anyone, the principal, Mr. Iago, comes barreling in, his bald head shining with sweat under the fluorescent light, a smirk on his face. He's a small man, not just in stature, and we have a history.

"Miss Heart," he says, "what did I tell you about coming onto campus and disrupting my school?" He gasps as he spots the worms writhing on the floor, then narrows his eyes at me. "What have you done to my staff? This is completely irresponsible. You will come with me right away." He reaches for me.

"Don't touch me," I say. My voice makes the room tremble.

Iago stops, frozen as everyone else. His mouth drops open. "How . . . how *dare* you?"

Before he can say one more annoying thing, Ursula zaps him. Mr. Iago shrinks and transforms, growing feathers in a rainbow of colors. "You gonna mess with my BFF?" she says. "I don't think so."

A few seconds later, Principal Iago hovers up and down in front of us, wings flapping.

"Nice," James says.

"Mary Elizabeth Heart," Principal Iago the parrot squawks, still the only one moving in the room, "you will report to my office at once."

"You couldn't turn him into something that can't talk?" I say, hands on my hips.

"Somebody get this guy a mirror," Urs says, her tentacles sloshing on the floor. "Or a cage." She cackles.

"Free!" James says, clicking the watch's crown, and the room reanimates.

"Your aunt," Ms. Aldana throws out, as soon as she can move her lips again. "She must be so ashamed."

The words land like uppercuts to the chin. Ursula watches them land.

CITY OF MAGIC AND MONSTERS

"Don't listen to her," she says as she grabs Morgie and we turn back to the windows.

"It's not what you think!" I call out to Ms. Aldana. "You'll see. We are doing it for the Scar!"

"They didn't care about us when we were at this school," Urs says. "They haven't earned the right to comment."

"Let's go!" Morgie's eyes glimmer with excitement.

"Chief!" James yells. "Please! Now!"

"Come back here immediately!" Iago screeches.

The glass fully dissolves, and after one last look at Ms. Aldana and the rainbow room we're leaving behind, we fling ourselves through the window. I feel like my limbs are being pulled off, that I'm being stretched to the point of breaking. I hold my breath as long as I can, and just as my lungs feel like they're going to explode, there's a huge flash of blue light, and James and I land with a thud—not in the chief's quarters like I was expecting, but in a place I would recognize anywhere.

The Ever Garden.

THREE

Magic slipped through the cracks, showed itself in tricks of light,
in butterfly wings, in creation of all kinds.

—*A People's History of the Scar*

MY HEART IS STILL POUNDING FROM THE CLASS-
room. I swear, I've never felt this good before, so right in my skin.
It's *amazing*. I squeeze James's hand to be sure we're still here
together.

Great ghost.

The principal is now a parrot, the security guards are worms,
but everyone filmed us, so the chief will be happy. We're no longer
missing, and no one thinks we're dead. Fears and suspicions have been
made real.

The villains are back.

I give an urgent glance up the one-way street, half expecting guards
to be following us, to have somehow chased us through the portal,
but there's no one. The street is silent, too silent, actually, and the
energy around the garden feels stale and sickly, like a plant that's been
overwatered and needs sun.

But we're here.

Outside.

At home.

For the first time since I took my reflection by the hand and traveled through my mirror, landing in Neverland, I can smell the outside air of the Scar, always with an underpinning of confectioners' sugar and the overcast coolness that has been present ever since magic came back and the long summer ended.

Even though the street feels abandoned, James pulls us behind a tree. "We need to be cloaked," he says. "We can't afford to be recognized now."

He whips a blue circle around us. "Think of something boring," he says.

"Boring? Like pancakes with no syrup?" I say.

"Exactly." The light flashes, then disappears. "Okay, perfect."

"You look the same to me," I say.

"But not to everyone else. I promise. It works."

"Okay," I say. "I trust you." And I do.

Now that we're safe, James strides over to the Ever Garden's gate. He dips his chin and scowls. "Those bastards," he hisses as he lets go of me. And then I notice. That's what's wrong here. The Ever Garden, always picky about who it allows into its woods, has crime scene tape all over its gate.

CLOSED UNTIL FURTHER NOTICE BY ORDER OF THE WATCH

FINE OR JAIL TIME APPLIES

James grimaces, his jaw working. "See what they've done?" he says, low and growling. "Vilifying magic. How dare they? They won't stop

until there's nothing left of our home. Well . . . not while I am breathing."
With that, he swipes his hook through the tape. He gives me a wicked
grin as he stands before the tall iron gate with the angels hovering over
its post caps. "That's better!" James says, and the air around us softens.
The Ever Garden agrees. "So what do you say, old friend? You going
to let us in?"

I slide up next to him, waiting to be accepted or rejected by the
garden, and for a second I wonder if the magic in the Ever Garden will
find us unworthy—if it, too, will think we're villains. Or maybe it won't
recognize us at all.

I read the inscription on the plaque that was mounted on the gate
after the Great Death. Like a half blessing, magic left us this one
enduring glimmer, and it is magnificent.

STEP THROUGH THE ARCH WHERE DREAMS ENTWINE
WHERE BLOSSOMS WHISPER SECRETS DIVINE
IN THIS ENCHANTED REALM YOU'LL SEE
THE LAST WONDERS OF MAGIC, WILD AND FREE

After a few seconds, the latch comes undone and the gate swings
open, and James gives a bow and sweeps me ahead of him.

As soon as we're through and the gate locks behind us, my body
calms. We're enveloped in magic, pure, sweet, kind, alive. The trees on
either side of us bow in greeting. "Hello, pals," James says, stroking a
weeping willow branch.

Before magic came back, this was its last vestige, a tiny trickle of what
had come before it, the place where magic felt safe enough to show
itself, where I saw the spinning blue light that's been with us ever since.

"Do you remember when we first came here?"

CITY OF MAGIC AND MONSTERS

"Yeah," I say as we step deeper and deeper into the understory. "'Course. Old Man Jenner had just gotten tossed out of here. The trees didn't like him. Everyone had been calling us names at school."

"I was 'the thief.'"

"They thought you had taken the milk money."

"And rumor had it you'd killed your family," James says.

"People are the worst," I say.

"Truly."

"So we came here together. We held hands. And we asked the gate to open," I say. "You told me if we were granted entry, it meant we were good."

James's mouth turns up in a wistful half grin. "Worthy. I said 'worthy.' *Good* is irrelevant."

"Right. And it let us in. We never got tossed out."

"No, we didn't."

"We felt—"

"Special," we say in unison. I let my head fall onto his shoulder. I feel the coolness in the air and a misty drizzle so light it's a tickle, and I inhale to soothe my lungs and parched throat.

"May I?" James says to a nearby rosebush, and it shivers, holding out a succulent red, heart-shaped bloom for him to pluck, which he does then presents it to me. "For you, babe. Welcome."

I take the rose, careful not to prick my finger, and glance around. "I've missed this place so much."

He nods.

We both know we're talking about more than the Ever Garden. We're talking about the Scar, too. It takes us a few more minutes to reach our special corner, which has a creek running through it. Everything here is a heart. It's not only the roses, the shrubs, the trees, and all the

42

flowers . . . the clouds overhead and the grass under our feet are heart-shaped, too, with lily pad candles swanning along in the water. On the weeping willow behind James, *J+M* is carved into the wood and glows in bright blue letters.

"Thank you, garden," he murmurs, as enchanted as me. "Thank you, magic."

I jump into his arms, wrapping my legs around his waist, feeling two hands cinch against me, drawing me in closer.

"If I'd known you would react like this, I would have brought you here weeks ago." His cheeks pink with pleasure as he releases me. The trees fold toward us, closing in the space and making us feel utterly alone in the best way. No one around to disturb us, no one to ask us for anything or need a question answered or check in about sleeping arrangements. I'm grinning so hard my cheeks hurt, the stress of the classroom far behind us. We're safe here. At least for now.

James leads me over to the creek, and I scoot down and dangle my legs into the chilly water. I lean back on my elbows and look up, and everything in me settles into calm.

"This is amazing," I say. "Perfect."

"I thought we could use some privacy," James says, taking off his boots and socks and settling in next to me. "So I got permission from the chief this morning to bring you here. I wanted to surprise you. I knew Monarch High was going to be as awful as it's always been, but I wasn't expecting all that. The guards . . ."

I shudder. I feel a little sorry for them, but Ursula gave them the chance to do the right thing. "Yes, agreed. And I love privacy with you," I say. "Anytime."

The glowing mushrooms beside us intone like chimes on a porch as the slightest breeze moves between them. James kicks his feet in

CITY OF MAGIC AND MONSTERS

the water, like he used to do when we were thirteen. That's the thing about knowing someone so long. You still see the younger version of them when you look at them and that's who shines through, no matter how many muscles they pile on top and no matter how many tricks they can do. The first time I noticed him kicking the water was the day his father went to prison for moving black-market weapons from the pier and for assassinating two people who threatened to interfere with his operation. James was a killer's kid, and my family had been murdered. That day, he had been sitting alone in the schoolyard. All the kids were splayed across picnic benches, under trees, everyone in clumps.

James was on the bleachers. I could feel him up there, radiating misery. His dad had just been sentenced, and everyone was keeping clear of him.

"You going up there or what?" Ursula asked, nudging my ribs as she followed my gaze.

Though it would take me a couple of years to know what it meant, James Bartholomew made me nervous, and that made me notice where he was in any classroom, any hallway, at any event. And of course, I had heard the stories.

About his parents.

About his dad, especially, who was in the same prison as the man who had murdered my family. Maybe I was supposed to hate him for that. I wasn't sure.

"You're staring, and it's weird," Urs said that day, pulling her new shiny black phone from her pocket. We were only twelve, and she was already herself.

I climbed the metal stairs where the football players did drills after school while he studied his shoes. As soon as I got close, I realized tears pooled at the edges of his lids.

"Hi," I said. "I'm Mary Elizabeth."

At first I thought he would ignore me. I prepared myself to turn around and walk away and never, ever talk to him again.

But instead he used his hand to shield his eyes from the sun and looked up at me, sniffling a little. "I know who you are. I'm James."

"Yeah," I said. "I know who you are, too."

He scooted over to make room for me, and I sat down. "Want to start some trouble?" he said, wiping at his eyes and forcing a smile.

I remember not knowing what to say, sweating under the hot sun and not being able to make myself leave his side. We've stayed like that ever since.

Somehow, between us, we found forgiveness.

"I have something to confess," he says now.

"Mmm," I say, ripping myself from my memories.

"I brought you here for a reason."

I scoot in closer so our bodies touch. "I figured. It's an elaborate detour."

He tents his fingers on the grass near the base of my back. "I think things are about to get . . . intense."

"Uhhh, I think they're already pretty damn intense."

"Fair point. But I mean, look at what just happened at the school. We all made it out, but pictures were taken. Choices were made."

"You mean Ursula transforming the principal and kidnapping him and also turning security into worms?" I perch my hands under my chin and bat my eyelashes. "Whatever would concern you about that?"

He smiles ruefully. "I mean . . . we'll get through this. But that's not

CITY OF MAGIC AND MONSTERS

actually what I'm talking about. I feel like by the time all this is over, that's going to seem like . . . like . . ."

"Like a walk in the Ever Garden?"

"Something like that. And, I don't know . . . I want to make sure you're ready. That *we* are. I want us to stick together no matter what, Mary. At the end of this—and the end is coming—I want us to be together, in charge, full of magic, and ready to live our lives . . . together."

I weave myself around him, listen to his heartbeat. "I want that, too."

"I just want you to tell me if there's anything you're worried about, anything you feel like I should know. Anything that might make this harder for us than it's already going to be."

"No," I say. "You're my love. You have *always* been my love. I still know what you're thinking before you say it. And I still feel as crazy about you as I did that first day we kissed."

"The night of the Fall."

"A terrible night for the Scar . . ."

"The start of everything for us."

We sit in silence for a few minutes. No one who was anywhere near the Wand that night can forget exactly where they were. Us especially. The Wand was the tallest building in Monarch and had been plunked down and built up in one of the green spaces in the neighborhood, which happened to be right outside my apartment veranda. James and I were out there watching the festivities unfolding on the anniversary of the Great Death, which is when magic disappeared. There were parties happening across the way. We could see people through the skyscraper's windows, all in glittering gowns.

"I'm going to take you to one of those parties one day," James had said, swinging his legs between the safety bars.

We'd only just decided to start dating, and neither of us had the gumption to kiss yet. But something about the way he said that gave me chills. I believed him, and I didn't believe anything anyone ever said. The world seemed built on lies. And yet I knew if there was any possible way James could do what he promised, he would. I leaned over and we kissed. Gia was inside and had insisted we stay where she could see us, so it was just a peck, but all my fears about kissing James evaporated.

The rocking shock of the Wand disappearing in a halo of jagged blue light knocked us right out of the kissing mood. The flash was blinding, and James cinched me in his arms, pulling my head into his chest. I didn't know what had happened. It took what seemed like forever for my vision to come back, and by the time it had, Aunt Gia was pulling us both to our feet.

For a moment—when I could finally see the place where the Wand had been, now an open crater, every last trace of the building gone—I thought we had done it. Our kiss was so powerful we had knocked down an entire building.

Of course, it would take time to understand how massive the destruction was, how many people had been inside, how horrible it was for those left behind never to know what had happened to their loved ones. Mally's mom was in that building. And the next day, water, oily and reflective, rose out of that hole. What happened the night of the Fall changed the Scar forever. We had already lost magic, and now it had risen up for more vengeance. But why?

It took a few more losses before Monarch understood how deadly that water was. All anyone had to do was touch it and they'd disintegrate. They called it Miracle Lake, but it always seemed like a beautiful monster's open mouth to me.

And it all started with my first kiss.

Now, James picks up a glittery pebble and chucks it across the water so it bounces, sending up tails of light. "I just want you to remember something, okay? When the Narrows come at us and try to take our magic away, *and they will*, we're still us. That's more important than anything else. Agreed?"

"Agreed." My pinky meets his hook, and we shake. I can't believe I once thought the solution to us being given Wrong Magic was an antidote to take it away. Lucas Attenborough gave me a vial of the formula his dad had made, and when I made it through the mirror and onto the ship, I panicked and hid it in my mattress. I was going to give it to James or figure out how to make more. It's still sitting there right now.

The antidote to magic is the last thing any of us needs.

"We're going to win this," he says. "If we don't, the Narrows government and those corrupt people at city hall are going to figure out the alchemy of magic and how simple it really is. They're going to steal it from us so they can control us. And it would be even worse if they caught us. You think you were experimented on before? If we're the only ones who can hold magic and use it, we'll be puppets for the rest of our lives."

"The Narrows are already taking over, making Legacy submissive. Shutting down our monuments, our history." I glower just thinking about it. "After the Great Death, the Scar was a total dumpster. And what did they do? Did they help us? Did they offer a hand? No . . . they took advantage, then they brought all their money in and dug for magic until they found it, no matter the cost for any of us." I shake my head. "That's never going to happen again."

James sucks in his breath and clutches his heart, biting his bottom lip. "Oh, you make me swoon when you're mad."

I swat at him. "Seriously. We'll see it through together. With the chief."

"With the chief," he agrees. "She's our best chance at having the Scar on top where it belongs. No more scraps. No more humiliation. We can get our dignity back."

"We can get our dignity back," I repeat, and we kiss. When we part I say, "I know you have questions about whether I'm really in, about whether I've really left the rest behind—"

"No," he says. "I know you—"

"Let me say what I need to say. Please."

"Yeah," he says, "okay."

"I wasn't sure about the chief, or about armies or experiments, or what she wanted out of all of it. And when Bella and I were trying to find Mally and Ursula, it was really looking like she was on the take, living some kind of double life."

"That turned out to be true," James says.

"Yeah. We weren't the worst detectives ever. We were on the right track. We just misunderstood. She was battling for us behind the scenes, and I had to get to Neverland before I could really see her for who she is."

"And that's a relief, right?" he asks. "You know . . . because . . ."

"Because she was the person who put away my family's killer?"

"Yeah."

"Yeah. I guess I need her to be the person I always thought she was, you know?"

"Yeah," he says. "'Course. And she is."

"I know. I'll never question who she is again, okay?" I let my forehead drop into the hollow of his throat. "I'm in . . . all in."

"Mare, I love you. You're my girl, because you've been my best friend since before Smee and all the boys. I owe you a lot."

"You owe me nothing. Just promise not to leave me again."

He sighs. "Why'd you have to bring that up? I had just had the magic. They were experimenting. The doses were all off. You know how it affected you. You practically split in half." He brings his hands into prayer. "I promise. I won't ever leave you again. You have to trust me. You do, don't you?"

The siren's song orchids start their swaying melody. It's said that their magic helps with creativity and invention, but it can also lull you to sleep. People have been lost here for days, and I feel myself swaying along with them, my lids getting heavy.

"It's so . . ." I mutter.

"Magical." James yawns.

"Beautiful."

"Perfect."

I see so many different parts of him, the layers of friendship and romance that lie between us. Warm and desperate eyes, the shell he clung to because his heart is melted butter and so many have let him down. I see us meeting for the first time, being the kind of friends who always defend each other. Our kiss the night of the Fall, how he's always been my greatest champion, aware of what I'm going through, and in spite of the part of him that has always thought like a criminal, he's been real.

As soon as I get back to the ship, I'm going to get rid of that antidote. Even if James never knows about it, I will. And once I do that I won't be hiding anything from him.

"You saved me once," he whispers. "Now let me save you back. Let us save everyone, together."

I have so many thoughts I can't quite catch. About his confidence in his own abilities, his greed, ambition, desires. James, my one and only. James, who is out to make the most of the magic we were born into.

He pulls me up to his mouth, meets my lips in a long, lingering kiss, then turns his attention to my neck, and goose bumps ripple across my skin. It's so good to be touched. I feel light as a petal floating on air.

"You brought me here so I'd forget everything else," I murmur.

"It's our place, Mare." There's a catch in his voice. I am reaching the depths of him, the still water that sits underneath. Here is the boy who was born to fail. Here he is, begging to rise. He completely relaxes. I wish we could stay here forever, the two of us.

James and I kiss again, lilies and roses curving around us, the grass shivering under our bodies. His fingers dig into my skin. I feel it all over but in my chest most of all, and when I open my eyes the blue light is back, circling all around us, brightening everything even more. This is the light that started it all, that first told me magic was back, that our lives were about to change forever.

"I trust you," I say. "I trust you, I trust you."

"I trust you, too, Mary," James finally says, speaking like he's coming from a dream. "I trust you forever." Doves circle around us, cooing their mournful song.

I sink into the feel of his body tucked against mine.

My Seed mark, which all Legacy are born with, quivers against my skin like a dormant creature twitching awake. The heart on my wrist burns as the siren's song retreats. It shakes me back to full focus. The light is waning above. It was midday when we got here. Now it's night, and the lily pad candles are more visible, glowier and showier against the darkness. I don't know how long we've been here, but it's far too long, considering what lies ahead.

"It's time for us to go," I say. "We'd better let the chief know she needs to portal us through."

He sits up, straightening, shaking himself loose from the spell. "I have a better idea." He clambers to his feet and offers me his hand.

I take it, and he pulls me up.

"You're going to portal us back." He cups my cheek and looks deep into my eyes. I start to protest, but he says, "You can do it. You know you can. I'm here. I'll help you. The garden will help you. Magic will help you." He pauses. *"You can."*

We stand over the water. The trees lean in, the orchids lean in, too, and the roses tremble. We peer into our wavering reflections. The blue light spins around us again, a magical hula hoop. "Take us back to the ship," I say. I don't fight, or panic, or dread anything. James rests his hand on my back. He is my past, my present, my future. He is my everything.

Within seconds, the light turns red.

"It's never done that before," I whisper, not wanting to disturb anything, for fear it will disappear.

"Red, for the Red Queen," he says. "You're incredible."

The air splits, then turns oblong. I catch a glimpse of water, a flag rolling against the sky, and I hear the sounds of celebration, leaking out to us from the ships. "James!" I say. "I think it's happening!"

"You're doing it," he says. "Keep going."

"I am a portaler!" I clutch his arm against mine. "I totally am!"

We are both giddy and free. "Goodbye, Ever Garden!" I say, waving. "And thank you." I smile, grab James by the hook, and pull us through.

We land on the ship, all our parts in place.

Everyone cheers.

* * *

In the early hours of the morning, when the ships are asleep, I slide out from between my sheets, kneel down at the side of the bed, and run my hands over my mattress until I find the tear I made to hide the antidote. I unwrap the red silk scarf I keep it in and hold it in my hand, gingerly as I would a bomb.

I roll the bottle back and forth in my palm, watch the liquid swirl with an illuminated viscous swish. Then I clasp it tightly.

I know what this means. This is my last chance of completely undoing the effects of Wrong Magic. I could take it myself, turn back into a good girl who does all the right things and doesn't question anything. I could get back on track to being the Mary Elizabeth Heart everyone expects, and life might go back to normal. I might go back to high school, then college for that degree in criminal justice.

I was going to be a detective and save other kids from having to go through what I did. That was going to be enough. And maybe I could have done that, one child at a time, one case at a time. Maybe that would have satisfied me, before I knew who I really was.

I would be abandoning myself if I did that now, leaving the Red Queen suffocated, gasping for breath. I'd be abandoning everyone else, too.

I stuff the vial in my pocket, then scurry up the stairs. I weave my way to the prow of the ship, my heart clanging.

The water is still and black.

Even in the dark, I can see myself on the ocean's mirrored surface when I bend outward. If I hadn't been brave enough to answer the Red Queen inside of me, I wouldn't have ever seen this place. Sometimes you have to take a chance. Sometimes you have to make a sacrifice.

Once certain I'm alone, I pause, the glass heating in my hand. When

I drop it into the water, the old Mary will be gone, once and for all.

I hold it outward and the ampoule teeters across my palm. I watch it fall, hit the water, and disappear. I pull back from the edge, hissing as my Seed mark burns hot and angry. I massage it with the thumb of my other hand. I expect to find it on fire. That's how much it hurts. But when I bring my wrist up to my face, it only looks a little redder than usual, the heart shape slightly more raised.

"Goodbye forever," I whisper to the old me. "And good riddance."

BELLA

NEXT DOOR TO MIRACLE LAKE, BELLA HURRIES UP the stairs of Mary's aunt Gia's cozy apartment building, the scent of incense and herbs wafting through the hallway: rosemary and lemongrass and a little patchouli. She is still learning the plant medicine that comes so easily to the Naturalists and marvels at the way they reach into jars and brew concoctions and spells. Her nerves thrum. They could get caught if the upstairs neighbors report the smell to the Watch, and the Watch is always . . . well . . . watching.

She uses her key to open the door and Gia meets her with a warm smile, her red hair pulled back in a loose ponytail, blunt bangs framing her face, wearing worn jeans and an emerald-green long-sleeve shirt. She scoots behind Bella and eyes the hallway, looking up, then down, before shutting the door behind her.

The Naturalists, Gia's group of friends who believe magic should not be forced back but should be naturally coaxed and wooed, are gathered around a cauldron. Silver in color, round and bulbous in shape, it bubbles over a flame.

Cindy, Evelyn, and Mattie couldn't be more different or more similar.

Cindy is tall and thin and is their de facto leader; Evelyn is short and curvy and is the sweetest of them, and Mattie suffers no fools. They've been friends since they were children, and it shows in the way they take up space, pressing their bodies into each other, and the way they all look up in unison when Bella arrives, like a three-headed creature.

"Sweetheart," Gia says, and pulls Bella into a hug. Bella doesn't mind it when she hugs her. Gia is special. Bella's been posted up in Mary's room for weeks, and even though it's nothing like the way Bella would decorate if it was hers, Bella sometimes can't wait to land on Mary's satin sheets and crank down the blackout blinds. But not tonight. Tonight she thinks they might almost have it figured out. "You made it."

The apartment is filled with an eclectic mix of modern furniture and mystical trinkets, a mirror on the wall facing the door. Mary's picture is plastered all over the place, and portraits of her parents and her sister are crowded in now, too, like Gia has to keep her ghosts close. A stranger would never know it's been years since Mary's family was murdered. They are so present here, Bella always has the feeling they might be coming around a corner any minute now.

Cindy slides her glasses up the bridge of her nose. They are foggy with steam. "Are you ready?"

"Where's Ginny?" Bella asks, looking around.

"Has a cold, poor thing," Evelyn says. "Shall we get started?"

"Would you let her take off her coat?" Mattie grumps, nudging Evelyn with her butt.

"But are you?" Cindy insists. "Ready, I mean?"

"Yes." And she is ready. Bella slides out of her coat and hangs it on the tree-of-life-shaped coat rack. She went to see Jasmine's parents today. They cried. It was long and sad and terrible. She is happy to be back here.

"Come come come!" Cindy commands, waving her over. "We don't have time to dilly or dally. We're ready to add in the gold. You'd better get it at once. Evelyn, fetch the Miracle water."

Evelyn is a potter, and she boiled down the gold in her kiln and added it to a clay pot so it will be able to hold the noxious water from Miracle Lake without killing anyone. Still, it's a delicate process. Evelyn reaches into the refrigerator, between the coffee cake and Gia's vanilla yogurt, and retrieves the urn-like vessel, holding it gingerly at arm's length.

"Great ghost be with us. I don't care for this type of stress at all," Evelyn mutters.

"None of that," Mattie says. "We've got to bring our Mary home." Mattie squeezes Gia's bony shoulder, and Gia nods.

"Ladies," Cindy says, "everyone put good energy into the pot."

Bella believes in plants, in logic and science and clues. She also has no choice but to believe in magic because she's seen it with her own eyes, felt it spark on her skin. Maybe there is something to the idea of energy, too, though Bella doesn't know how to add it to a spell.

"You should do the honors," Gia says to Bella.

Evelyn hands her the water. "We've got blue lotus, rosemary, laurel . . . all the herbs for psychic communication."

Ah, so Bella was wrong about which herbs she was smelling after all. She makes a mental note to learn.

"All we need now is the water and the Seed marks," Cindy says, moving the cauldron from the stove and onto the old pine coffee table in the center of the living room. "Light," she says, snapping a finger.

Mattie and Evelyn and Gia retrieve long tapered white candles held in silver sticks and set them up in a circle formation. They light each one.

"May the circle be unbroken," Gia says.

CITY OF MAGIC AND MONSTERS

"May the circle be unbroken," they repeat.

Aunt Gia adds a few dried petals and the mixture emits a soft glow as it swirls together. The air hums, sending tingles down Bella's spine. Something is happening, and although Bella isn't certain it's the desired result, this is far better than nothing.

"Ready, ladies?" Cindy says.

"Born ready," Evelyn says.

"Well, we all know *that's* not true," Mattie pipes up. "It takes learning and practicing, especially considering magic has been on the run and might not be in the mood at all—"

"Not now, Mattie!" Cindy booms.

All five women hover over the brew.

"If we die," Evelyn whispers, looking around the circle, "I love you all very much."

"*Tsk,*" Cindy says.

The room settles. It's so quiet it feels like the apartment itself is listening, arcing toward the women.

When Gia gives her the signal, Bella tips the water over their wrists, using her right hand while her left stays over the pot. As it touches their skin, the hearts on their wrists, blue light begins to spark.

"My gods," Mattie says. Five blue hearts rise and meet over the pot, glimmering and sparkling, swirling and whirling. "We didn't die, Evvie!"

Bella feels sick even as the other women giggle and exclaim.

"All right, ladies," Cindy says. "The spell!"

"Remember," Gia says to Bella, "we only have one chance. There won't be another new moon for a month, and it's a month we don't have. This has to work."

"Oh," Evelyn says, swooning at the ball of light like she is no more than three years old. "Remember when we were little and we could magic all day? Weren't those the times? It's been *thirteen years* since the Great Death. So long. So long. We didn't even know what we had . . ."

"Shhhh," Mattie, Cindy, and Gia say in unison.

Bella might vomit.

Everyone focuses in. The atoms in the air sparkle. Bella has memorized the spell, and she hopes every word does its job. They have gone to so much trouble.

"Now, as you say it, send light and love and joy to Mary," Gia says.

"So pretty," Mattie whispers, then slaps her free hand over her mouth. They all hold hands, in a semicircle, and stage-whisper the words they've constructed so carefully, and that they all know so well.

With gold's light and magic's might,
We call upon the Legacy of the night,
Bring Mary Elizabeth home to me,
Safe and sound, so must it be.
Mary, come home
Mary, come home
Mary, come home

They say it all again, then one more time. The light swims through the air between them, stopping to pirouette, then plunges into the cauldron. The mixture glows and flashes before flattening to a dull gray. The women look, one to the other, unsure what to do next

"Well . . ." Gia says, breaking the silence.

"Did it work?" Bella says.

"*Something* happened," Gia says. "I felt it."

CITY OF MAGIC AND MONSTERS

"We'll just have to see," Evelyn says. "Only time will tell."

"It worked," Gia says. "Sometimes you have to have faith. Mary belongs here with us. Magic will bring her back."

After the candles are blown out and the pot is emptied, Bella excuses herself to Mary's room while the others clean and gossip and try to cheer Gia. Bella sits at the edge of the bed as she kicks off her shoes. On the dresser is a framed photo of Mary Elizabeth and Ursula and James Bartholomew, dressed up for an event, maybe a school dance. They are young teenagers. Mary is in the middle, and James and Ursula hover over her protectively. Mary is muscular and small, both at once.

As she does every night, Bella reaches into the top drawer for a lighter and sets flame to wick. She doesn't know how she feels about the great ghost or hope or fate, but she puts palm to palm and looks into Mary's eyes. Mary, who lost her parents and sister; Mary who wanted to be a detective but has become something else; Mary, who is so driven by loyalty to her friends that she is blind. And then, Bella prays.

Please bring Mary home. Please bring Mary home. Please bring Mary home.

Even her prayers are spells, now. Outside, the Scar is quiet, nervous from its sidewalks to its hedges to its majestic maple trees.

Bella gets to her feet, removes her socks. Between trying to find a way to contact Mary and searching for Jasmine, Bella's feet are tender, bruised, and covered in blisters. She's going to have to soak and bandage them. She'll need them to be in top shape tomorrow, when this starts all over again.

She flops onto the bed and finds her phone, dials one of her starred contacts. It rings once, twice. Then someone answers.

"Hey, it's me," Bella whispers, to be sure the Naturalists can't hear her. "We need to meet. I need your help."

FOUR

It was only when the first Legacy was born, the first mark on
the first wrist, that magic emerged, awoke, and took flight.

—A People's History of the Scar

THE NEXT DAY WE PRACTICE WITH THE VANISHED
for so long we almost forget about Morgie's welcome ceremony,
and when the chief summons us, we are all spent. Her table is bare
except for five candles, a bejeweled knife, and one bottle of liquid magic, and Morgie couldn't be happier. She circles the setup,
exclaiming about how lovely the bottle is, *ooob*ing and *aaab*ing.
Mally and Hellion lurk in the shadows, Urs is watching her carefully, and James hovers nearby.

We all remember what it was like to work with magic for the first
time, to feel it. Though we're careful and have learned to start out small
so we don't run into people growing horns and tentacles, it's still fun
to watch someone else join in, but also . . . it's magic we're dealing in,
ancient and moody and unpredictable, with a personality, a will, and a
set of rules we don't quite understand.

Morgie runs a finger along the outside of the bottle. "I am completely

CITY OF MAGIC AND MONSTERS

ready." Her eyes slither over the candles and she turns to Urs, her body tight and straight. "Am I going to be like you? Will I . . . transform? Do I get tentacles?"

Ursula raises an eyebrow at Morgie. "I'm gonna be me and you're gonna be you. You're going to be the person you would have been if the Narrows' leadership hadn't ruined everything, trying to use magic to make themselves rich, before the Fall. Remember that."

"This is going to be *amazing!*" Morgie says. "Whatever it is."

Mally hisses.

"What's the matter, Mal? Too much excitement for you?" James says, scooting in next to her.

"Enthusiasm makes me uncomfortable," she says. "Gives the universe an invitation to stomp you."

"There she is. Right on brand," James returns, nudging her with an elbow. I think I see the glimmer of a smile on Mally's face, but it's hard to tell from here.

"Well, hello!" The chief glides down the stairs in a blue silk cocktail dress with a red pendant at her throat. She's used to hobnobbing with elite society in Monarch and I think she misses it, so she's always ready for an excuse to get dressed up. "Welcome, Morgie. We are so excited for you to join. Smee showed you your room, and I trust everything was to your liking?"

"It was perfect," Morgie says, swooning. "I love the floating hammocks."

"They're good, aren't they? Protect from any seasickness."

"Yes, ma'am."

The chief rests hands on hips and smiles. "I believe in happily-ever-afters. We are so excited for you to be here with us, and we hope this is the start of yours." She huddles in next to Morgie like it's just the two of them. "In the days before the Great Death, when Legacy joined a coven or any society, they took a blood oath. We feel it's important to continue the tradition."

Morgie licks her lips like she's about to be served a bleeding steak. "I'm so here for it."

"Well," the chief says, "looks like we're not going to have any trouble with you, are we?"

"Never," Morgie says.

I remember the first time I accidentally portaled into Kyle Attenborough's secret lab when Urs and James and Mally were being held captive. The empty bottles, not as nice as these ones, had held the liquid that was used to experiment on my friends. Now we use what's in the air here in Neverland, the magical water from the lake, and our own blood to make the magic we need. Morgie won't become a monster, but she will never be the same as she is now, a regular human.

"Mary," Ito says, "why don't you do this one?"

"Me?" Ito always does the blood oath. "I . . ." I hesitate, but then say, "I'm honored." Flashes of Morgie as a little kid run through my head, bright, loving, playful.

Urs has gone back to picking something out from under one of her nails, and I imagine Morgie long ago, showing me paintings she made at school. She always idolized us, and we shut her out. Now is our chance to make up for that.

"Okay, honey," I say, stepping up beside her. "You ready?"

"The most ready anyone has ever been for anything!" Morgie puts her hands behind her back and teeters on her tippy toes.

The light from the candle flickers.

"This'll be over quick, okay? You'll take the oath, then drop the potion on your Seed mark. This makes you one of us, forever," I say. "I promise it's going to be okay. It only hurts for a second." I pick up the blade. "It's a tiny cut."

"I'm not scared," she says.

I put out my hand, and she places her delicate fingers in my palm. So trusting. "You're special, Morgie. Not only are you like a little sister to me, the chief has decided after this we're complete. You're the last of the Vanished."

She steadies herself, takes a couple of breaths, and says, "Okay, I'm ready."

I reach for her ring finger and prick it as quickly as I can. She lets out a sharp exhale. "When we move as one, with the blessing of magic," I say, repeating the chant we always say when a new Vanished joins us, "we are unstoppable." I take the blade and slice the pad of my own finger, then press it against hers. "Now together."

"When we move as one," we chant, "with the blessing of magic, we are unstoppable."

I take our combined blood from the tip of my finger and let it drop onto her Seed mark. "Now you alone," I prompt.

"When we move as one," she says, barely above a whisper, "with the blessing of magic, we are unstoppable." The air crackles in the cabin as I pour the bottle over her mark. It's only a couple of drops. The blue liquid meets the blood, and it turns a purple that matches her lips. Then, as though the Seed mark is a thirsty plant, the liquid absorbs into her skin. "And one drop for the spirit of the heart of magic," I say, and drip a tear's worth of potion into her wound. "This seals your commitment, and ours."

It feels right that Morgie should be my inductee. And I thrill a little, because over the last few days I have really felt the chief beginning to lean on me as a leader. I imagine when we take over Monarch she won't have time to do everything herself. She'll need us to be her captains.

Once the ceremony is over, we all wait to see what will happen. After Stone's ceremony, he could sing like an angel and play the guitar like a demon. For Flora and Fauna, wings sprouted from their backs and wands appeared in their fists, and they began casting spells to green up the ships and bake the most delicious cakes. It's always different.

"Is it going to work?" Morgie says, searching us for answers.

"It will," the chief says.

For a moment I'm afraid my blood is not as powerful as the chief's. But then Morgie trembles, and her eyes turn a catlike yellow. "I see," she says, as if from miles away. "I can see everything." She flings herself into my arms, then rushes over to Ursula. "Thank you! Thank you all so much for coming to get me. Thank you."

She makes the rounds, embracing everyone except Mally, who offers her a pat on the shoulder instead.

"Magic acknowledges and accepts your agreement," we say in unison when she has settled down. "You are one of us. Legacy Loyalty."

"Legacy Loyalty," she says solemnly, sending up purple sparks from her fingertips.

When they've all gone upstairs and the chief and I are alone, she says, "You did a remarkable job."

"Thank you," I bloom under the light of her attention.

"You're extraordinary. Look what you did yesterday. You brought life to a dead room. You portaled and brought yourself and James back safely."

CITY OF MAGIC AND MONSTERS

"The Ever Garden had something to do with that."

"Maybe. Maybe not." She blows out the candles one by one. "Maybe it just gave you the confidence you need." She pinches the final candle's wick and gathers them up. "Someday you'll be where I am now."

I pause, balancing the empty bottle and scabbard. "You think . . . I could be like you?"

"I do," she says. "I know a queen when I see one."

"Thank you so much, Chief," I say. "Just . . . thank you for everything."

Magic.

It's not only spells.

It's family, too.

Sunset is a sherbet tonight, and the party is afoot. By the time I get on deck, there are so many people it takes me a minute to find James playing pool with Mally and Urs standing next to the stage. Mally pounds the eight ball into the back right pocket, dour as ever.

"You like my new pet?" Urs asks, and she cocks her head toward a gleaming cage near the entrance to the main cabin. Principal Iago.

"You did not," I say.

"Oh, but I did." Sure enough, I see eyes gleaming from inside the cage and a rainbow of parrot feathers.

"You're not going to leave him like that, right?"

Urs slurps the sugar off the rim of her pink drink and swings her hips to the beat. "Eh . . . we'll see how I'm feeling. If he behaves, I *might* let him out. For now, I'm kind of liking how quiet he's being, after all the years I had to listen to him babble."

Tonight, the boats have been magicked to sit still as Popsicle sticks frozen in ice, and Stone plays a guitar spelled so its sound ricochets off the water like it's amped. Bodies flail and pulse in a wave. The decks of the *Legacy* and the *Loyalty* and the others are in similar shape. Joy bubbles to the surface, overflowing.

As I'm surveying the scene, Wibbles turns Damien Salt into a kangaroo.

"Epic!" he says, before charming him back into his normal muscular self. "Thanks for letting me practice on you."

"Anytime, my friend!" Damien takes a moment to adjust back to being in human form, then, noticing me watching, charges over and wraps me in a giant hug. "Mary, Mary, come join the festivities!"

Tucked into a corner, the Lost Boys have pungent tea, and sweet rose-covered cakes are delivered on a pulley system. This last lot is placed on a table set with a red tablecloth and bedecked with petit fours and macarons.

"I made elderberry cream–filled pastries, and I didn't even use magic at all." Damien beams at me and pulls at my elbow, excited to show me his creations. If anyone else touched me like that I'd curse them into a puddle and mop them into the sea, but Damien is my friend, a real one. As we reach the table, Damien scoops up a cup of tea and waits for my nod before adding in some cream. "Have something to eat!"

"Don't mind if I do!" I sit at the table and the Mad Hatter plants himself across from me, helps himself to a plate of brightly colored cookies, and pours some tea for himself. He's got a paperboy hat on tonight and rubs his tattooed arms before taking a bite.

"What do you think?" Damien asks, watching Hat and me anxiously. "You like the food, or what?"

"Perfect," Hat says, taking a bite of a pistachio macaron.

"Great job, D," I agree. "When we get out of this place and back to the Scar, you've got a future at the Layer Cake."

"You really think so?" Damien says.

CITY OF MAGIC AND MONSTERS

"Sure! You've got so much experience now you've been cooking for everyone."

"No," he says. "I meant . . . you think we'll make it back to the Scar? Like, to live?"

"Of course we will," I say, and I rest my hand on his forearm.

"It's just . . ." He lowers his voice. "Sometimes I don't know if I want to go back. Sometimes I hope we stay here forever. I know I'm not supposed to feel that way, but I do."

I know what he means. Here on the ship, it's like we're in another time, so far from reality and all that it brings.

"You feel what you feel. And don't worry too much. Once we win back the Scar, we'll be free to use magic. We can come and go as we please. I bet the chief will let you come back here whenever you want." I squeeze his forearm. "Really."

"Yeah," he says. "I hope you're right."

It's dark now, and party noises ring into the night. The amount of people hanging from the sails is alarming. Flora, Fauna, and Merryweather are dancing again, but this time a few feet off the ground, charming each other bouquets of pink and blue flowers.

"Fireworks!" James says, bounding over. The navy-blue night is peppered with flashing lights that double on themselves, spin, and fly, changing shape as they go. "Isn't it beautiful?" James says, hugging me around the waist.

"Gorgeous," I say, leaning against him. I think of Lucas Attenborough then, how he climbed into my room the night his father died and told me he thought I was better than my friends, that I had more heart. I wish he could see me now and know just how wrong he was.

"Look! There!" James points directly overhead, and more of the kids run to the edge of the ship to see what's above, hands thrown over shoulders, delirious and ecstatic. The fireworks take shape, spinning lights into snowflakes, crystals, a huge and rotating moon. They separate into letters. For a dizzy moment I don't know what they say. But then I see them clearly:

COME HOME NOW MARY
WE NEED YOU

I blink, once, twice, three times. The letters are still there. "Do you see that?" I ask James, frozen in place.

"The tea-set fireworks?" James says. "Of course."

"No, not that." I point. "The words?"

James scans the sky and shrugs. "What words?" He leans back and looks in my eyes. "Hey . . . you okay?"

"Yes, it's nothing," I say, hugging his arms closer around my waist. He kisses my neck, then rests his chin on my head.

James would overreact if I told him I was hallucinating again, like I did when the Red Queen was playing games with my reality. Or . . . what if it's not that at all? What if it's a real message? That would mean someone could somehow communicate with me here in Neverland. And *that* would mean something could be wrong.

But what if it's a trick? What if the people in Monarch are trying to draw me out?

"Mare, seriously. You look like you saw a ghost," James says.

"It's fine." With effort, I regain control of my breath. We won't be here long now. I'm not giving up because of a few words written in the sky. I couldn't be happier. I'm with you, aren't I?

James studies me, before he goes back to staring upward, and I'm grateful he can't read my mind. Everything is okay. Everything is great.

The next time I set foot in the Scar I'll have a whole army behind me. And it will be war.

FIVE

At first, the citizens of the Scar didn't know what was
happening. Whole worlds were opening before them,
worlds they did not understand.

—*A People's History of the Scar*

"WHAT'S GOING ON, HONEYBUNCH?" URSULA ASKS,
peering up at me from the water, a soft smile sneaking across her
lips. "You look like scrambled scallops."

I spent the night watching the shadows on the ceiling, listening to
the creaks and whines of the ship, thinking about that message in the
sky summoning me back to the Scar, and took a chance on finding Urs
awake before anyone else was up. I checked her cabin, which was empty
as usual, her stuff in a series of friendly piles on the floor, boots and
heels scattered across the carpet. When I didn't find her, I checked the
next logical place. The water. And I am so happy she's here.

"You just going to stand there?" Urs says. "Come on down, cookiepuss."

"I didn't sleep," I offer.

I creep out onto the plank the Vanished like to use as a diving board when they want to play in the ocean. I flop down onto my butt and let my legs dangle.

"I didn't sleep either," Ursula says. "It was such a perfect night, ya know? I didn't want to miss a second of it. Just me and the moon and the stars and the water. I'll take myself a little resty later." As she talks, she circles in the water beneath me. She's graceful and strong, her tentacles muscular knives slicing through the surface. "Don't be so intense all the time. That's my philosophy. Life is about having fun, causing mayhem, keeping things interesting. The world is what it is, so you might as well party, right?"

"Yeah, might as well." I scoot forward a bit so I can see her better. "I could go for a night at Wonderland, though. A little Dally Star action. Some cards or a game of croquet."

"I bet you still have the record on that game."

"Probably not. I bet some freshman Narrow has taken number one."

"You kiddin'?" she says. "No one is as committed as you. And no one is as good." She pauses, gray skin glinting with moisture. "So, what's on your mind?"

I don't want to tell her about the message until I know how I feel about it, but just being here with her is making it all a little better, my thoughts finally settling down. "Do you remember when you went missing?" I say, after a bit.

Urs nods. Of course she remembers.

"I thought you were dead."

"I wasn't."

"That's good, because I'd be lost without you."

"Yeah, you too, kid."

"And then there was the night James and I found you, when all the rumors first started in the Scar about a sea monster?"

"I found *you*," she says.

"That's when I knew nothing was ever going to be the same again. I wanted to pull you out of the water. Rescue you."

"Ha," she says.

I meet Ursula's eyes. "If James and I had gotten you out of the lake, found help, maybe we could have gone back to being kids. Magic would have faded into nothing. You ever want that?"

"You kidding me? First of all, I never would have let you get me, toots. I would have slid right through your fingers. I wanted magic, not Frappuccinos and history and high school. I didn't want to learn about the past, I wanted to live in the present." She shakes her head. "You always liked the world more than I did, Mare, wanting to be a cop and everything. The system was never for me. And besides that, I already had the magic by then. There's no going back from that. You know that's true. You tried."

Ugh. Just thinking about those weeks trying to keep the Red Queen at bay gives me the willies. I was so alone and confused.

"Back when this started, all I could think about was getting magic. I was as bad as Morgie." She grunts. "I thought all I had to do was sign up for this little program Lucas Attenborough was selling at school. I knew he wasn't any smarter than me, so whatever he was up to, I might as well find out how it could benefit me. Us. He's got all the money. All the status. All the power. What did he want with our crew? I thought maybe there was some chance that spoiled little rat wasn't totally full of it, that he would have something to show me and I would be able to steal it. Either way, he suckered me in, and I couldn't get out."

"Tale as old as time."

"Yeah." She snorts. "Maybe I'm not as smart as I think, eh?"

"You are—"

"Nah," she says. "I'm not. But it doesn't matter because I got what I came for and I'm not sorry. I'm glad I did it."

"So . . . why were you at the lake that night? You never told me."

"Oh, that?" She shrugs. "I escaped Kyle's lab and jumped in thinking I might as well end it all."

My throat thickens and my heart twists. "Urs—"

"I was having wild thoughts and didn't know what else I could do. I only knew I was half fish, and I didn't want to live my life in the bay. But I didn't die, even though Miracle Lake was supposedly made of the deadliest poison known to man."

"No, you didn't."

"You know what I did instead?"

"Went swimming?"

"Yeah." She leans back into the water. "And it was heaven. And I could feel, I don't know, the whole universe. I could feel how powerful I was, too big for my little human body."

I remember Ursula, tall as a building, towering over the Scar, looming across Desire Avenue during the Battle at Miracle Lake. That's how much power she really has. But I can only imagine what she's been through. The time I accidentally portaled into Kyle Attenborough's lab, I thought I had landed in hell. The torture chair, the notes on the desk rating different pain thresholds. They must have suffered. No wonder they don't want to talk about it.

"You don't care what happens to the Scar," I say. "Do you?"

"Why should I?" she says. "What did the Scar ever do for me? Took my magic. Took my dad. Might as well have killed my ma." She shakes her head. "Nah. We're better off here. When this is all over, I'll get my mother, my sister, and we'll live somewhere special together. I have just the place. I've been getting it ready."

"Like, on the ship?"

"No, not on the ship, silly." Before we were here, Urs had her little black book, her secret burner phone, all her deals, promises, exchanges. Now, she has magic. So it must be somewhere magical. "The chief and I have an understanding."

"What kind of understanding?"

"I need to be free and I need a place for my family, and the chief needs . . . other things. Quid pro quo. She gives, and I give back."

"But—"

"Hey, sweetie," Urs says, "it's the same as it always has been. Way better for you if you stay out of it." And just like that, the window into Urs's life slams shut. Curtains drawn. Lights off. Blinds down. Subject change. But then she softens, seems to change her mind. "Come under the sea with me," she says. "Let me show you something."

"Under? I can't," I say. "I'll drown."

"No, you won't drown." A devious grin appears and she takes the necklace off and holds it in her palm. She blows on it, and it snaps open. A perfect, clear bubble sits at its center.

"You're going to use this," she says.

"What am I supposed to do with it?" I ask.

"You just sit back and let it happen." Urs floats the shell up to me, and the bubble pops out into my palm. It feels like glass, heavier than I expected, but then it grows and grows and grows until it's as big as me, and with a snap, it's around me, jiggly and opalescent. "What does this do?"

"You'll find out," Urs says, and with a flick of her wrist, she sends me over the side of the boat.

"Okay," I say as I float down to the water, "I'm trusting you."

"As you should, cookie. As you should."

CITY OF MAGIC AND MONSTERS

I go under, and for a second everything is a blur of blue and green. I hold my breath and wait for water to choke me. I kick against it, at the mercy of my instincts, trying to get back to the surface. But I'm not drowning, and I don't need to swim, so I relax, one breath at a time. The bubble follows Ursula like it's on a leash as she goes down, down, down. I don't feel any pressure from the dive as we sink lower and lower. Urs gives me a thumbs-up as we pass an octopus and a lot of seaweed, and the water goes darker and darker, before it begins to lighten again. It's like we've passed through a black velvet ribbon, only to wind up in water that's a bluer blue than I've ever seen, that clear, crisp kind I used to dream of when I read travel magazines, and the sea life gets friendlier and sweeter looking as we fall and fall, eventually landing on the finest white, diamond-like sand. I'd imagined if we dove into the water and went deep enough, we would end up in the Scar again, pop up in Miracle Lake. I didn't think there would be this, a landing pad, much less a whole new world.

The bubble finally pauses next to a giant skeleton. Out front, eight rainbow-colored creatures stand guard. They're small but look like they could do a lot of damage.

"Good job, youz," Urs says as they part ways to let her through. "Mantis shrimp. Nothing like 'em. They look cute, but they'll punch right through you. I turned Flotsam and Jetsam into eels, too. Ma's too sick to take care of 'em, and they're good extra protection." Flotsam and Jetsam are Ursula's cats. Were. They don't look like tabbies now as they appear from behind the skeleton, undulating at Ursula's side.

I feel the shrimps' eyes on me as I pass by and go deeper into the monster's belly. It's dead now, and bigger than our entire ship. Ursula beams.

"How great is this? My very own leviathan." Urs shows me the inside of her house, where a manatee is cleaning the sand with its snout. Everything is festive, from the mermaid candlesticks to the tricorn hat sitting atop a bust of Medusa. Old furniture is charmed to the floor, and she's even got a coral coat rack. It's just how she likes it.

"No wonder you're hardly ever topside anymore," I say, running my fingers along a satin sofa with gold embroidery.

"Maybe not topside, but the chief lets me go visit Ma as much as I want, as long as I don't look like me. I guess she doesn't want any more reports of sea monsters in the *Genie's Lamp*. C'mon," she says, winking at me.

Farther inside the skeleton are trunks full of gold and jewels. Furniture that must have come from an old shipwreck. She's got a closet full of clothes, too, all hanging, magicked to look dry. She even has a portrait of me, her, James, and Smee outside the high school on the first day last year.

"A life away from the riffraff," Ursula says. "You think it's magical up there in Neverland? Can't touch this. We got mermaids, sea serpents, talking stingrays. And so. Much. Treasure. It's the most."

"Swanky for sure," I say. As I follow her, I note there's a working kitchen, and even lights. She glides delicately around the space, humming to herself as she spins a record on an old gramophone. I've seen Ursula dominate and I've seen her having a lot of fun, but until now I don't think I've ever seen her comfortable, like she's exactly where she's supposed to be. "Shipwrecks everywhere. So much to gain. I've got a garden out back and . . . oh, I don't know. I just wanted you to understand. I'll go back to the Scar to fight so magic can be alive and well again, but I won't be staying there, and I always want you to know where to find me."

I look out through the leviathan's tail and spy a little garden filled with different varieties of seaweed, swaying in the water. As I watch them through the murk, I realize what they are: the living seaweed I saw bunched around Ursula when I first got here. When I asked what they were, I remember, James said, *Loyalty. They didn't have any.* And I shudder. But also, there are so many. The garden stretches endlessly behind Ursula's secret sanctuary, for what looks like acres.

"Are you going to take me back there?" I ask, curious, but not sure what I want the answer to be.

"Nah," she says breezily, pulling me away from the window. "It's not ready to be seen. But I'm working on it, and when it is, I'll show you."

She pulls me into her living room, then lounges on an old pink chaise and sighs happily while I sit down across from her, the bubble widening its protective orb to encircle me and my chair. The manatee floats by, continuing to vacuum her floor, and a sea urchin rolls alongside us like a tumbleweed.

"So, what do you say?" she says, smiling blissfully as she reaches into a nearby drawer. "Want to tell me what's going on with you?" She pulls out a deck of cards and starts shuffling. "Talk over a game of hearts like we used to?"

"Like we used to," I murmur, watching her deal a pile on my side of her shipboard coffee table.

So long ago.

Almost like it never was.

SIX

Some could fly. Some could grant wishes. Others could transform and transmute. But perhaps the most mysterious of magics was that of the portaler, for whom time and space would bend and fold, and for whom none of the rules seemed to apply.

—A People's History of the Scar

WHEN WE GET BACK TO THE SHIP, THE BUBBLE shrinks down and I put it back into the shell without any trouble. Ursula squelches on deck beside me, dripping. I remove the necklace and hand it to her, but she waves me off.

"You keep it."

"Really?" I say, feeling its ridges.

"Well, yeah, honeybee, I want you to come see me again." She sighs contentedly. "What do you say? Want to come back down and visit your old girl from time to time?"

"Of course . . . if everything goes well in the Scar."

She arches a brow. "Oh, it's going to go well." Her smile grows. "They're not even going to know what hit them." She takes the necklace out of my hand and fastens it around my neck. "So you can find me if

CITY OF MAGIC AND MONSTERS

you need me." She blows me a kiss, and with a leap, she disappears over the side and hits the water with a graceful slap.

The Vanished are taking direction from Smee, cleaning the benches, wiping down the waterproof cushions, setting the table. Only instead of using washcloths and getting down on hands and knees like they usually do, they're shouting out commands, charming buckets, ordering pillows on benches to fluff themselves.

I'm on my way down to find James when a hand grabs me and yanks me into the only corner there is on deck, behind the entry to the magic room.

I jump into a fighting stance, my fists shooting up, ready for a quick spin and cross jab, when I hear a hissing "It's me!"

"Mally?" I say, turning to face her. "Get your hands off me."

"With pleasure," she says. "As soon as you put your hands down." Hellion is on her shoulder as usual, and he watches me severely. He could peck my eyes out. "I just needed to get your attention."

All around us, a shimmer cascades like an opalescent waterfall, blurring the outside world. Mally holds her staff in its center as light pours out in all directions, her hood pulled high over her horns so she looks deep and shadowed as the dark side of the moon. I'm so close to her I can feel her breathing.

"What's going on?" I ask. I'm unaccustomed to being this close to Mally. She smells like woodsy amber, and her skin is smooth, poreless. "What do you want?"

"I saw you go into the water with Ursula. The bubble she gave you . . . Where is it?" She speaks urgently, quickly, like time is at her back, pushing her forward.

I don't know why she would want the bubble, but it's probably not for good. I feel a protective surge toward Ursula. She's got her home down there, her peace, finally, after so many years of suffering. I'm not about to take that away from her by giving Mally Saint access. "I don't have it, and even if I did, I wouldn't give it to you."

She narrows her eyes as I feel the necklace press against my skin under my shirt. "Fair," she says, then takes a deep breath and looks at me square. "I'm a vengeful person. A petty one. Prone to tantrums. I am spoiled and privileged, and I have never been kind to you. I know all that." She uses her free hand to pull back her hood, exposing her face. "Which is why you should trust me when I say I would never come begging at your door unless I had to. I need it. I need to find a way to get to the bottom of the sea."

I consider. "Well, I don't know what I can do about that. Go ask Ursula."

"Come on," Mally says. "She hates me."

"*I* hate you."

She smirks. "No, you don't."

I groan in frustration. "Okay, I don't. But you are very annoying."

She twists her mouth and waits.

"You want to go under? Tell me why."

"I *need* to."

"Because?"

Mally growls. "None of your business."

I tap on the gooey protective dome. "Can you let me out of here?"

"No. Not yet. Will you listen to me?"

I don't respond.

"My dad is missing, and he always liked you."

Her dad is missing? But he was the mayor of Monarch. Where could he have gone? Jack Saint and I were friendly after Bella and I helped find Mally, back when no one knew where she was. Mally and I were connected, and he knew it. He knew I'd be the one to bring her back, to find her and rescue her. I don't think he expected me to bring her home with horns, able to shapeshift into a dragon, to be permanently hunted in the Scar.

"I always liked your dad, too," I admit.

"Then can you trust me?"

"I trust Ursula. Why don't you magic yourself a bubble if you want to go into the water?"

"I would if I could." She strokes Hellion's feathers. "I can't. I don't have any power in the water. I've already tried."

Mally presses her lips in a flat line, then blows out air. "I'm not part of your friend group." She waves her hand over her staff. A picture appears. My family, walking together in Midcity, my sister Mirana tripping through the snow. I bite my lip to keep from crying out as I see Mira holding my father's hand, swinging it back and forth. "But we do have some things in common," Mally goes on. "I lost my mother in the Fall. My father is all I have left. If your father was somewhere and then he was nowhere, wouldn't you want to find him, too?"

"Yeah," I say, feeling my heart lurch, a knife always stabbing that I can never explain to people who don't already understand.

"You know what it's like to be an orphan."

My mother's scent comes back to me in waves of bergamot and lavender. "Yeah, I do."

"That makes us sisters, if only in this one way."

I reach for her elbow, but remember how much Mally doesn't like to be touched. This time, she gives me a plaintive look and settles her hand in my hand as though she's been waiting for someone to dare to be skin to skin with her, even with her tiny, knobby joints. Neither of us pulls away.

"You're not an orphan," I say. "No matter what, you have us. Even if you are a truly unpleasant person."

"Right back at you."

We let our hands drift apart, the silence thick between us as the cleaning extravaganza continues outside.

"So, what does all this have to do with Ursula?" I ask her.

"Maybe nothing. Maybe everything."

"Mmmkay . . ."

"We have both lost everything. We are both vengeful. And I think we can help each other." She leans in. Hellion chitters. "Get me to the bottom of the sea. I'll explain everything to you then."

"Yeah," I say, "okay. Why not? You and me on an outing. That'll be nice and weird."

She smiles, briefly, and except for how much it looks like it's hurting her face to do it, the expression seems almost genuine. "Meet me here at midnight. Ursula is still sleeping on the ship, so she won't be under the sea. I promise it'll be worth your while."

I nod, feeling a little sick at the idea of Mally in Ursula's sanctuary. "I'll see you then." She stands up tall again, satisfied. "But, Mally," I say. "If this is some kind of trick or test, just don't. Because I won't forgive you, and I won't stop until I've settled the score."

"Yeah." She snorts. "I'm terrified. Midnight?"

"Midnight," I confirm.

Her face relaxes. "Stay safe, and don't tell anyone. Not even James." She straightens and draws back.

The protective shimmering spell disappears, and she slinks off like she's walking the runway.

Fairy dust. This is a mess.

SEVEN

While bakers experimented with laughing pancakes and love
lollipops, one family was discovering whole universes.
They were the Spades.

—*A People's History of the Scar*

AFTERNOONS ARE FOR PRACTICE AND ENCHANT-
ments, and while Smee and the rest of the Lost Boys are trying
out new spells and defensive magic, we're reviewing our strategy.
Mally, me, James, the chief, Ursula, and the Mad Hatter, always
at the chief's side. There is no tea. There are no crumpets or petit
fours or tartlets. The only overhead light is on, illuminating the
table with its giant map of Monarch, which plays out our plans in
animation.

Mally taps her fingers on her staff with Hellion nipping at her ear.
She shows no signs of having approached me and scrutinizes the map
as the chief paces back and forth, spinning her finger so the figures on
the map move locations, then move again. Finally, she stops and looks
up. "James, your briefing, please."

"We're teaching the Vanished some last defense exercises using the tools we should be able to use in the Scar." He reads from a scroll. "We have the amulets that reflect the attacker to themselves, confusing them; bows made from phoenix feathers that never miss their mark; and shields that protect the wearer. Flora and Fauna are producing enough wands for everyone to have extra in case any break."

"Good," the chief says. "Let's shore up our offense as well. The plan is to portal simultaneously into police headquarters, the mayor's office, town hall, and into the city itself." She points to each location on the map. "Those who go into the Scar will be charged with peaceful demonstrations of magic. After all, the hope is their families will be so happy to see them, they'll be too overjoyed to worry about the ridiculous anti-magic usage laws. What do you have to report, Ursula?"

Urs looks at the chief, heavy-lidded. "I shapeshifted into a couple Magicalist meetings and a villain fan club meetup, and they're so hungry for magic, they're exactly where we want them. A rebellion is going to be no problem."

"Mally," Ito says. "You and Ursula will be in charge of zapping any heavy hitters. I think if you shrivel a few people the rest will cower, but you never know. The important thing is to show the world that we come in peace but are ready to fight if attacked. We have every right to magic openly." She sidles over to me and lays a hand on my shoulder. "And you, Mary. Your job is going to be to portal us in and out, so you need to practice until you're confident. I will open them, but then you will have to hold them until everyone can get through. And if there's an emergency . . ."

"I need to portal them back out," I say.

"Because you'll be storming city hall," James says to the chief.

"*We'll* be storming city hall."

"Yes," James says. "Can't wait." He grins, his hand on his hip. "Once the fairy dust settles, we'll party all day and all night, magic everywhere, and we'll have ice cream for breakfast, too."

"I was thinking justice, peace, and equality," I say, and James shoots me a grumpy look.

"I didn't mean those things won't be happening," he says sullenly. "I'm just saying we can have some fun while we're there."

"All right," Ito says, looking satisfied. "We have to get there first, in one piece, all together." The room grows quiet. Things could go terribly wrong. I could fail at holding the three portals open at once.

"Okay," the chief says. "Everyone head upstairs. Mally, get those fairy shields going strong. Mary and James, you focus on making the magic. Hat, please see to defense."

"Aye, aye," James says, and we all disperse.

James and I are in the magic room, surrounded by *DRINK ME* bottles and the red ribbons we wrap around their necks to signify that they're full and ready to go. I've taken the opportunity to think about the message in the sky last night, and to mull over Ursula's lair and Mally's request to be taken there. I don't think she has bad intentions, but something is not sitting right about any of it. That, coupled with the news that Jack Saint is missing, has me on edge.

I prick my finger with a golden needle and ease out a drop of blood, let it meld with the magic in the bottle, which hisses, and wonder again whether I should tell James about the underwater garden and the meeting with Mal. James has always been the person I share everything with.

"You seem quiet tonight," I say when the blood has properly blended with the water and the gold.

"It's Saturday," he says after a moment. His hook clunks to the table as he pushes a new set of bottles over to me. "Monday we march on the Scar, and . . . I'm feeling different than I thought I would."

I look at him more closely and find him wan, more tired looking than I've seen him since we got here. I abandon the bottles and go over to him. He brushes his hook over my cheek.

"What is it?" I say. "Different how?"

"I guess I've enjoyed it here." He gives a wry smile. "It's silly, I know . . . but I like the ships and the laughter and the magic, and I love the training, too. I like being with my people, here on the ocean, without buildings and a society that doesn't work, and without thinking about my parents and the Scar, worrying about something broken instead of looking ahead to something I can build the way I like it." He sighs and strokes my hair. "I want to be free."

"You don't think we're going to lose, do you? That they'll lock us up?"

"We're definitely taking a risk," he says. "The second we cross over into the Scar, all this will be gone forever. If I had the chance to explore what this world really has to offer, I might stay on the *Mary Elizabeth* and lead this crew forever. I want us to be young, beautiful, and powerful just like this until the end of time. Once we're back on solid ground, anything could happen."

I take hold of his wrist and kiss its seam. "So you don't want to go home?"

"Do you? Back to the worry?"

I have known from the moment I got here that we were going back, that the whole point of us being here was to return. Staying here is not anything I've ever even considered. "It's been a vacation from the life we've always known, but it's an in-between, not the thing itself."

"I know," he says. "But sometimes I think I'm a swashbuckler at heart.

It would be so fun on the high seas, with the boys, forever." His eyes flash with excitement at the thought, and I have to admit I can see him on the open water, hanging from the flagpole. He makes a face and rubs his hook, mischievously. "All I need is a good adversary."

I laugh for a second, but then I realize he's actually serious. Like, *serious* serious. "But the chief . . . she needs you. And I couldn't stay here. Not long-term."

"Of course. But once things have been corrected in the Scar, she's going to have plenty of people who will want to join her. She'll have her pick. And don't you think she'll choose a grown-up when the time comes?"

"I think she cares about you. She's not just going to cast you aside. And besides, we're almost grown-ups now."

"Maybe," he says, shrugging. "But I've never felt the way I do here, like anything is possible. And after Monday, I might never feel that way again." He lets out a ragged laugh. "Oh well. Who cares, right? It is what it is. Who gets to live a whole life being a kid, hanging out with friends and playing pirates?"

Sometimes James is a lost little boy. Like now.

"Hey," he says. "Everything's good, right? I'm sorry I'm griping. I want to be with you, okay? You above everything else."

"You above everything else," I say, my fingers tingling against his spine. For the first time since we found each other, I wonder if James is being honest about how he feels. He may have found something he wants more than me. "Us against the world," I say, wanting it to remain true forever.

"Yes," he says. "Us against the world."

He cinches his arms around my waist, and I calm.

One night, when I was at my internship at the Monarch City Police Department, I did a search. I knew, even as I typed my father's name, Aaron Heart, into the database that nothing good was going to come of it, but I couldn't resist.

The crime scene photos came up immediately and without warning. My mother on the floor in a pool of blood, face covered in a blanket like the person who stabbed her didn't want to have to see it, her hands shredded with defensive wounds, visible lacerations all over her chest. My father on his stomach like he was crawling to her, knifed in the back, his gray hoodie soaked dark. And Mira. Only five years old, blond and thin like my dad.

I don't ever want to feel that kind of loss again. And I don't want secrets between us.

"James," I say. "I have to tell you something."

He furrows his brow, puts the bottles down, and folds his arms across his chest. "Okay."

"Last night, when I asked you about the fireworks, if you'd seen anything in the sky—"

"Yeah?"

"I saw—" But before I can say anything else, the drums start up, signaling it's time for dinner.

"You saw . . ." he prompts.

Barnacle bounds in and leaps into the space between us as Smee pokes his head through the door. "Youz coming to eat or what?"

"Is this important, or can we finish this conversation later?" James says. "I'm starving."

"Yes," I say, burying my hands in Barnacle's soft fur. "Later."

* * *

CITY OF MAGIC AND MONSTERS

It's a long and boisterous dinner. The Lost Boys take turns giving speeches about the glory that is coming our way when we march on the Scar. Pleading a too-full belly, I go to my room, inhaling the scent of the roses climbing my wall.

"Clock," I say to the heart-shaped timepiece on my bedside table, "wake me up after midnight."

"Midnight, ma'am?" I animated Clock when I got here, and he's a little fusty. I'm not going to tell him my business, but he looks like he wishes I would.

"Actually, quarter till. Okay?"

"Yes, of course, ma'am. Only, you need your rest."

"Yes, Clock." I smile. "I will rest."

Even with the noise coming from upstairs, I fall asleep quickly and deeply, exhausted.

I wake up in my room. Not my room on the ship. The one in the Scar, at my apartment with Aunt Gia.

Home.

And Mally is beside me.

She's sitting cross-legged on my black comforter. She looks how she used to, no horns, high black leather boots to her knees over black leggings, Seed mark climbing her neck. She's watching me, waiting for me to see her there. I have missed my room, with its pictures and candles and books. I've missed my pens and the journal I used to scribble in, and the sound of Gia in the living room . . . the sweet smells of lemon custard cake baking in the oven. It's as though I'm really there. But I'm not. I know I'm dreaming.

Because I've had this dream before.

Or almost, back when this all started. Back when Mally was missing.

"I have a present for you," she says. "Don't squander him."

90

A caw so loud it shakes my bones ricochets off my walls. I raise myself up on my elbows, the world wavering around us like we're underwater.

And then we are.

Water is everywhere, soaking my sheets, my clothes, climbing down my throat.

I don't drown.

I can breathe.

I have a bubble.

Help, Mally whispers. *Please help me. Mary, please help me.*

"Time to get up, Miss Mary. Time to get up," Clock says.

"Okay," I say, breathing hard. "I hear you. Thank you."

I am drenched in sweat. I flip on the bedside lamp and pat Clock on the head. He returns to the corner of the side table and, after a moment, shuts his lids.

The ships rock on the water, silent, so I sit in one of the deck chairs to wait for Mally. When the sun begins to rise, I go back to my room, churning with dread.

EIGHT

Mermaids appeared on the beach, animals spoke, and the rest of the world began to take note. "What," they asked themselves, "are we going to do about what's happening in the Scar? And more importantly, how can we benefit?" They rubbed their greedy palms together and began to plot.

—*A People's History of the Scar*

I WAKE UP TO A KNOCK ON MY DOOR.

"Come in," I say.

It's Smee, his mouth pressed into a straight line, his body tense. Barnacle barges past him and hops on the bed, demanding pets. I sink my hand into his brown fur. He pants, looking up at Smee adoringly. "Sorry to bother you. The chief told me to gather everyone."

"Did she say why?" One glance at Clock tells me it's only six thirty in the morning, which means I didn't sleep much at all.

"Nope," Smee says. "Probably wants to hype us up or something."

"Okay then. Grab me some coffee and I'll meet you up there."

"Will do," Smee says. "Come on, Barnacle, you big lug."

When they're gone I brush my teeth and splash some water on my cheeks, my Seed mark buzzing on my wrist. Something is definitely up. I climb the stairs to the main deck. All the Vanished are out and at attention, along with the Lost Boys, minus Wibbles and Damien Salt. I wedge myself between James and Smee, on the stage where Stone and his band play. Smee hands me a warm cup of bitter coffee. Ursula is there, too, in full human form, and Hat stands on her other side.

James casts a worried glance my way and offers me his hook to hold. I take it with my free hand. The *Legacy* and the *Loyalty* float nearby, decks filled with children, all whispering to each other about why we're here, while Flora, Fauna, and Merryweather float, wings fizzing in the air around them.

Barnacle sits down at James's heels. I scan the crowd, taking inventory of all the bodies. "James," I say, finally, "where is Mally?"

I don't see Mally anywhere. It's one thing for her to have stood me up last night and another for her to be missing now. I finish off my cup of coffee, instantly wishing I wouldn't have. My stomach turns queasy and I magic the cup away as the chief comes into view.

She struts forward, dressed in a white jacket with epaulets and straight white pants. This feels awfully official, the way she used to dress when she was the chief of police. Damien and Wibbles are behind her. Each of them holds one of Mally's elbows, and as she follows the chief onto the stage with the rest of us I see that she is bound with a black rope, wet and slick, that slithers across her mouth.

Only it isn't rope at all, but snakes, black and oily and glinting.

"What the hell?" James says under his breath.

The chief turns and looks at Mally solemnly before speaking in an almost intimate tone. "After everything I've done for you, my heart is broken."

Mally's eyes go purple for a moment, and I expect her to set the

CITY OF MAGIC AND MONSTERS

chief on fire, to blast the snakes off her, to unshackle herself. Of all of us, Mally is the least likely to go gently. But nothing happens. Her eyes return to normal. Her shoulders soften, like she's yielding to her fate. She has no staff. No Hellion. Only her horns remain, sharp and glinting.

"As you can all see, something horrible has happened." The chief faces the crowd, sweeping her arm outward. "One of our dearest and best leaders has betrayed us." The murmurs rush over the ships again and carry out across the water. "Mally Saint is a traitor," Ito says.

"Traitor?"

"Traitor how?"

"What did she do?"

I catch the snippets of conversation like snowflakes in midair.

"I know . . . I know," the chief says. "It's shocking, and I wanted you all to see, to hear, to witness. We're a family, and this is going to be very difficult for all of us." She heaves a mournful sigh, and her face twists into anguish. She lets the silence splay out as worried children clutch their own shoulders and lean into each other with wide, bovine-like eyes, waiting for whatever is next. Finally, she speaks again. "It has come to my attention that Mally Saint has been plotting my demise."

Whispers scatter through the crowd again.

The chief raises a hand to quiet them. "But that's not all. She has been communicating with the false leaders in city hall and has alerted them to our plans. Because of her, our entire enterprise may be in jeopardy." She nods. "Magic may never return, and our people may continue to suffer."

A disgruntled murmur starts up.

"Now, now," she says. "I'm doing everything I can to find out what's going on. I have people in Monarch, and we will find a way to fix this.

But first"—she takes Mally's elbow, pulls her away from the boys—"we must make sure that Mally Saint doesn't do any more damage."

I look to James, but he's not watching me. His mouth is dropped open, pain etched on every feature.

"If she had been allowed to move ahead with her plot," the chief says, "reaching out to those who would work against us in the Scar, more harm would have been done, and all our families and everything we value would have been lost to us."

James can't take his eyes off Mally. She cinches her mouth even tighter as Ito pushes her forward. A cheer rises up, the crowd jeering and yelling about Legacy Loyalty, about one for all and all for one.

"You kiddin' me?" Smee whispers. "She's gotta do this in front of everyone? Poor Mal."

"Maleficent," Ito says. "You are charged with treason." Mally narrows her eyes. "Now it's up to you. Do you want to let the traitor have any last words?"

"No!" the Vanished yell in unison.

"Mary," the chief says, turning toward those of us on the stage with her, "you are a loyal person. You have always been a loyal person, fighting for what's right, defending those who need it, working hard for the benefit of those you hold dear." She lays a hand on my shoulder. "Maleficent has two main sources of power. One is her staff, and the other is on the top of her head. We have taken possession of her staff, but in order for us to be safe, we must remove the latter. Therefore, I am giving you the honor of cutting off Mally's horns."

The chief and the Mad Hatter exchange a look and in a flash he's before me, hand extended, the blood oath dagger balanced in his palm.

When terrible things happen, time slows down, gives you time to absorb every awful second. That happens now, as the blade glints. This isn't a story. We aren't characters in someone's imagination. We are real. Mally is real. I could make a portal, let her escape across the world somewhere. Or . . . *maybe* I could.

Mally doesn't fight. Her face is unreadable as she sinks to her knees and bows her head to me. I cut off James's hand to save him. I could justify that. He would have died if I hadn't. Mally's horns were once a sign of the monster she had become, a physical manifestation of what the Wrong Magic did to her. But now they seem so much a part of her I can't imagine her without them.

I can't move. I only stare at the dagger in the Mad Hatter's hands, eyes flickering back and forth between the chief and him, frozen in place as if I had been turned into one of Ursula's worms myself. I feel the panic rising as I think about Mally, who she has always been: a mean girl, rigid and cold and arrogant. I think about the vision in her staff of my family, of her mother's demise, of her father's proud and loving face. She does not deserve this.

As the seconds tick by, an uneasy, pregnant hush has fallen over the boats. Even Iago is quiet, watching from his cage. Everyone knows this is a flex. Mally is capable, and she's being taken down in front of two hundred witnesses.

"Now, Mary Elizabeth Heart," the chief says. She waits. The Vanished shift around uneasily. "Do this."

When I stay still, her face falls. "Or have I overestimated you?"

Mally looks up at me, the awful, beautiful sister I never wanted. "I can't," I whisper.

A wave of acute displeasure falls over the chief, like the face she has pasted on—the one filled with joy and kindness—can no longer hold purchase over the fury she feels. Her forehead smooths, her lips pinch, and her jaw tightens.

"This is your last chance, Mary," she says, "to do what is right for your compatriots."

"I'm sorry," I say, with a hesitation that makes me hate myself. "I just can't."

"You can't?" the chief says, arching an eyebrow high with disbelief. She takes her time, each word deliberate, consonants emphasized. "That doesn't work for me at all."

My stomach curdles with dread. The Red Queen has abandoned me. I can hardly breathe as pieces try to connect, itches I can't reach.

"Doodly-doo, I'll do it for you!" the Mad Hatter sings, startling me with his fervor and the loudness of his voice, which echoes across the water. He stuffs the dagger into his back pocket. "I owe you for getting me out of that horrible jail cell, don't I, Mary Sue?" It's the old nickname he had for me when he was in prison, when the Red Queen took over and broke him out.

"Thank you, dear Caleb, for helping to protect this ship and all its precious children," the chief says, softly.

The Mad Hatter bows. The first time I ever heard of him, he had his cronies dropping body parts in gift boxes all over the Scar. I thought he had something to do with Ursula's disappearance, and he did, just not in the way I suspected. Should I be grateful to him now?

Mally twists her neck, wincing, tears dripping down her cheeks. The air is thick with our fear, like a tsunami is coming and the animal in all of us wants to head for higher ground. But there is nowhere to go.

We all have to watch.

Caleb pulls his meat cleavers from his holsters. "Close your eyes, Mal. I'll be quick."

He spins, raising his arms high above his head, and with one swift movement, he slices the cleavers through the air, guillotine-like, cracking bone with so much force and with such sharp blades that Mally's horns fall to the ground instantly.

The Mad Hatter collects them and bows as he hands Mally's precious horns to the chief.

"Your loyalty will not be forgotten, Caleb," she says.

The chief snaps her hand around the horns and shoots me a reproachful look before turning her attention back to Mally.

"I am so sorry you chose betrayal, Maleficent. Sorry you have left us with no choice but to take extreme measures. It pains me as if you were my own daughter."

Mally turns away, refusing to look at any of us any longer. I take a step back, my knees weak; everything weak.

The chief pulls Mally to her feet.

"I take no pleasure in this," the chief says. "Mally, you were the first one for whom magic worked, the first to feel the power and responsibility when it emerged from its deep and terrible slumber. It's because of you that we're all here today. Magic reawakened in you, and you betrayed it." The chief lets the moment stretch out. "Mally Saint, for the crime of treason against the people of the Scar and against magic itself, and for breaking your blood oath to the Legacy, you're hereby sentenced to death by drowning."

Death? Murder? Treason? Beside me, James tightens, ready to spring. Whatever he does, the others will follow. I'm sure of it. I steady myself, braced for a fight.

The chief hangs her head sorrowfully, then sheds a single tear that glimmers in the sun. "I'm very sorry it ended this way. I wish it had been different. May the next life bring you better luck and better choices than this one. You will be mourned," Ito goes on, "not as you are but as you could have been. Not this cowardly shell, but as a gifted dark fairy. Now ... walk the plank."

The plank she's referring to is a long board attached to the ship. Without a magic bubble or protection spell, anyone who falls from that height with hands bound would be dead and drowned as soon as they could no longer hold their breath, and Mally can't move her arms at all. I never thought the plank would be used for anything more threatening than late-night starwatching.

Mally strains, showing fear for the first time, cranking her neck to look at me. Then, stumbling, she wrenches away, and when she meets James's eyes, she seems to calm. I understand. James has that effect on me too. A safe harbor even in the worst of times.

All his muscles are taut. She understands he means to intervene. I catch the slightest shake of her head. I catch something else, too. James has been lying to me, or at least not telling me the whole truth. His feelings for Mally are as clear as our reflections on the water beneath us. Mally gives him one last, fierce look, and turns her back to all of us. She climbs onto the plank, graceful even without her arms to support her. When she reaches the edge of the board, she turns around.

It is utterly silent on the ships. She stares straight at James.

She never takes her eyes from his.

Not as the chief raises her hand.

Not as she sends a lightning strike of magic that crashes against Mally's chest with the force of a speeding truck.

I feel the tendril of attachment between them, even as Mally's body hits the water.

No one tries to stop her fall or goes to her defense or tries to magic her out of the situation. Those of us who have known Mally our whole

CITY OF MAGIC AND MONSTERS

lives, Ursula and James and Smee and the Lost Boys and me . . . we abandon her when she needs us most. All of us stand in silence while the frenzy mounts around us, feet locked to the boards.

I wish I had given Mally the bubble. My hand reaches for the bump of the necklace under my shirt. But still, I don't move. I don't help. I am not a queen at all.

Mally can't use her arms or legs to keep herself afloat. Water will be filling her lungs now, choking her as she falls into the murky darkness with nothing and no one, facing her death alone.

Mally, who laughs like someone who has never known joy, who may not like me, but who would never stand by while the same happened to me. Ito would have been a pile of ashes if she had been in my place.

Mally Saint is . . . was . . . a much better person than me. I will never forgive myself for this.

Never.

Everything blurs: the Legacy Loyalty flag, the blue-green ocean, the flock of flamingos standing on a sandbank in the distance. It all comes undone in my mind.

"This," the chief says, "has been a most unfortunate turn of events." She clasps her hands solemnly and addresses the silent, frightened children standing on the decks of all the ships as her ruby glimmers in the sun. All the fun, the magic, the leaping and playing and lightness . . . it's all gone now, disappeared along with Mally. I can practically hear all the thoughts teeming through the air around me, the Vanished asking what they should do now and how any of us will ever go back to normal.

I can answer that: We won't.

No one speaks or dares to look away from the chief. The party is most definitely over.

100

The chief addresses the crowd again. "I hope you all understand that had to be done to keep us safe. Your safety is my primary concern. So," she says, turning her gaze on me, "as long as no one here is putting anyone else in jeopardy, that will never need to happen again."

I grind my teeth to keep from saying something that will lead to more calamity, but I don't look away from her. Her eyes, which I have always found so beautiful, are the dead, predatory black of a shark's, and her mouth turns up menacingly. The message is clear. I have disappointed her beyond repair by defying her in front of everyone. The chief calls out to James, who is hovering uncertainly on the deck.

"A moment of your time, please," she says.

The Vanished begin to whisper to each other as I pass them by. I see the questions on their faces, and the dawning realization that this whole thing is not a joke. Someone has died now. "How do we get out of here?" someone whispers as I walk by. I feel hands on my forearms, see looks of panic everywhere.

After weaving slowly through the crowd, I glance behind me to make sure the chief and James are still in conversation, and when I see her arm patting his tensed back, I decide it's time to take my chances. My legs move faster beneath me as I careen down the stairs and head for my room. Once there, I slip into my steel-toed boots, tie on my knife sheath and dagger, and twist my hair into a bun, then let out a heavy sob.

Just one.

But Mal.

I have to find out what Mally wanted at Ursula's.

NINE

After two generations, the Spades had mastered the art
of the portal. They had learned that the lineage passed through
its daughters and was driven by emotion, which could either
help or hinder the degree to which they were able to move
through the world, and indeed, worlds.

—*A People's History of the Scar*

AS SOON AS EVERYONE GOES THEIR SEPARATE
ways, I climb down the rope ladder so I don't make a splash, and
when I'm a few feet away from the water's surface, I snap open the
shell necklace. I let my hand rest in the air above the tiny bubble.

"Come on, Bub," I whisper. "Take me back to Ursula's."

The bubble shudders, stretches into an oval, rolls out of its shell with
a pop, and grows until it's big enough to cover me.

"Thank you," I say from inside its protective embrace. I slide into the
water, dip beneath the surface, and begin my slow descent. I trust that
the bubble will hold me against the pressures of the deep and I know
I'll be able to breathe, and so I am not afraid as I was last time.

I am haunted by the thought of Mally's torturous drowning, that she drifted down this same path. I couldn't bear to see her corpse, and I pray that the water will take us on different paths, that I don't have to look into her vacant eyes and see what I already know . . . that all my judgments about her should be turned on myself.

I am the one who is wicked.

I slide down through a school of jellyfish, past a grinning shark and her baby, and through the dark ribbon that leads to the world down there. For long, lonely minutes, I am steeped in a blackness that's only broken when an angler fish passes me by, its snaggly teeth in a horror-movie grin. Without Ursula's yellow eyes to help lead the way, I have to remind myself that this part of the journey won't last, and I won't be stuck in this deprivation tank forever.

As the darkness becomes the sky above and I get close to the sand, it's obvious I'm not in the same place as last time. Ursula's house is nowhere to be seen. I'm the only person on a lost highway. This is not ideal, but at least my fears about Mally are unfounded. Her body is not here. Not anymore, at least.

But now I have a new set of problems. It's possible I floated off course. Or maybe, without Ursula, the bubble doesn't know where to go. That would be worse.

"Bub," I whisper, "we need to go to Ursula's. Which way is it?"

A nudibranch and a giant leafy seadragon float by, creatures I remember from biology. They appear to be in conversation, and they pay me no mind.

I am watching them disappear when I hear, "Excuse you!"

The voice is high and tinny, and I spin around to see where it's coming from. I find a woman with a green shell bikini top and a green tail to match. Her hair floats behind her, lifting and rolling through the water. Her tail flits like a blinking eyelid.

MERMAID!

No . . . mermaids.

With hair every color of the rainbow, a half dozen of them bob up and down like seahorses, each one of them staring me down.

"I said, excuse you," the green one repeats. She taps on my bubble, which I don't like at all. "Can you hear me in that thing?"

"Hello." I remember learning in class that mermaids like people to be deferential and appropriately amazed by their existence, but not too over the top or they might attack. I nod my head in a slight bow. "My friend told me you exist, but I haven't seen a mermaid in person since I was little. I have always wanted to see a mermaid again. And now here I am. I'm honored." They continue watching me, but they do seem less hostile. "Where I come from there haven't been mermaids since the Great Death."

"What's the Great Death?" the blue-haired one says.

"Oh, it's . . . well . . . magic died . . ." I try to explain, but it's immediately obvious they have no idea what I'm talking about because they roll their eyes, laugh, and nudge at each other, sending bubbles up toward the black.

"Magic can't die, silly," the blue-haired one says.

"You would think that, wouldn't you?" I say. "It's doing fine here."

"Hmph," the green-haired one says. "Well, I'm sorry, because you seem like you're probably a decent human, but you'll have to go back up and turn in your bubble. Those have been illegal for years." She swishes her tail. "We don't allow your kind down here. Not after the harpooning incidents. Pirates cut out our tongues and sold us on the black market. They called it big-game fishing. Do I look like a fish to you? 'Sustainably sourced,' my fins!"

"The point is," the blue-haired mermaid says, "you gotta go."

"Bye, now," the one with pink hair says. "Come on, girls. If we don't hurry, we're going to miss the party."

Before I can say anything else, they roll me across the sandy bottom, spinning me like a terrible amusement park ride. I'm on my third rotation when I remember I have magic, and I send an electric shock everywhere they're touching the bubble. They fly backward, the water around them fizzing angrily. I get back to vertical and give them all my meanest glare. "My name is Mary Elizabeth," I say. "Otherwise known as the Red Queen."

"You don't look like a queen," the one with blue hair says.

"Yeah. Though . . . she seems kind of powerful," the pink-haired one returns.

A mermaid with long black hair and puffy red lips comes from behind and leans in. "Why are you down here, Your Majesty?"

"I'm looking for my friend Ursula."

This stops them. "Ursula the sea witch?"

That's the perfect name for her. "Yes," I say. "I'm looking for her house. Her skeleton. I'm her best friend."

"I'm Attina," the black-haired one says. "This is Alana, Adella, Aquata, Arista, and Andrina. Any friend of Ursula's is a friend of ours, right, girls?" Alana and Aquata agree but keep their suspicious eyes trained on me. Attina says, "Come on." I follow behind her, rolling along as gracefully as possible, and after a minute I get control of the bubble and charm it to ride smoothly behind the mermaids.

"We love Ursula down here," Attina says. "She looks out for us."

"Yeah," Aquata says, "there were these mermen who were being totally inappropriate with us, wouldn't leave us alone, and she turned them into weeds!" She giggles, but I don't think it's funny. My detective senses tell me something is in Ursula's backyard that I have to see. I've known since I got to Neverland that Ursula keeps her shriveled-up adversaries somewhere, and my guess is that they're in her backyard. I also suspect that's what Mally was interested in.

What I don't know is why Ursula wouldn't let me back there. Which makes me wonder *who* she's hiding.

"Oh, don't get upset about it. They deserved it, trust me," Attina says. "And now maybe the mermen will think before they mess with us again."

"We still travel in packs. It's really not safe down here unless you're in the kingdom, and even then, you should always have a buddy. Between the sharks, the giant squids, the tentacled beasts, and the sea monsters, we need protection around here, and sometimes we have to get out of the palace, you know what I mean?" Adella strokes her shark-fin mohawk. "You're lucky it was us you ran into. That's all I'm saying."

"But if Ursula is your best friend, then you'll be fine. No one's going to cross her."

"Here we are," Attina says as we approach familiar ground. We stop in front of the leviathan, and I have never been so happy to see a carcass. "You want us to wait?"

"No," I say. "I can defend myself." I show them a zap of red light between my fingers. "Thank you for showing me the way."

"Tell the sea witch the mermaids say hi," Adella says, and they swish off, disappearing into the distance.

Without their tinkling voices and glitter I am utterly alone. The mantis shrimp guard the front door and don't move as I walk by them, but as soon as I round the corner, I spot Flotsam and Jetsam floating in front of the garden.

"Hi, boys," I say, imitating Ursula's voice as best I can. "I just need to get past you. Here, kitty kitty." Flotsam and Jetsam stop, appearing confused. They circle me but back away. "Do mama's babies need a little walkie-poo?" I inch myself forward and they follow, swishing and sliding back and forth, gliding up to peer straight at me. I try not to notice their cat claws or the way they lick their lips. Urs and I used to wonder whether if cats could eat us, they would. We should have asked what they would do if they turned into mutant cat-eels with electric powers. They pause before lunging for me, ready to strike. I hold up my hands, and in a flash, I've deanimated them and they sink to the ground, turned to stone. "Sorry, boys," I say.

I waste no time. Up top they'll be looking for me soon, and I need to see if my hunch proves out. I rush through the gate and grimace. This is no ordinary garden.

No wonder she didn't want me to see it.

Instead of finding seaweed or a collection of plankton, I find row after neat row of worms. Only these worms are not ordinary. They are planted in the ground, and they have eyes.

Human eyes.

As I roam the manicured rows of misery, I spot a familiar cluster and lean in to see more closely. They look exactly like the security guards from the school after Ursula cursed them. I never gave another thought to what happened to them once we were gone. Ursula must have brought them here. Ursula . . . or the chief. Urs said she had some kind of agreement with Chief Ito. A place to be free in exchange for something she didn't want to talk about. Or couldn't.

The whole garden seems to be leaning toward me, pleading.

I force myself to roll through each row, looking into as many pairs of eyes as I can. There must be thousands of them down here. It would take me forever to acknowledge each one. I feel like I owe them some form of connection, though, especially knowing they're here, suffering in a state of compressed consciousness, with no way to free themselves.

I've always been obsessed with eyes. The colors are spectacular, greens with flecks of gold and rings of blue, brown eyes with surprising shades of red. I love the way James's flash and Urs's brown ones go gold when she's feeling crafty. The eyes are not only the windows to the soul, they're the windows to the storms raging inside.

I reach the center of the garden, drawn by one particularly fleshy gray blob. Its eyes are brown, birdlike, and beam with intelligence. I gasp with recognition and back into the edge of my bubble.

No. It can't be.

And yet it is.

I lean closer. They brighten as I near, filling with something like hope.

It's Jack Saint. Mally's dad. The mayor who was in business with the chief and who helped me understand what was happening. He must have gone against her or gotten greedy. He lost his wife when the Wand disappeared and now his daughter is gone, too. Maybe he's better off here. But gods . . .

This is the deal Urs has going with the chief? That anyone the chief doesn't like can wind up here? I look out, to row after row of swishing seaweed. I don't know what I've become anymore. It was okay when I could imagine that all them were terrible and horrible and deserved to be transformed into nothing, but now that I know Jack's down here, I wonder who the rest of them are. How many enemies does the chief have? And how many will I have if I march on Monarch by her side?

I can't trust the chief at all, and she's about to drag my friends down a very dangerous path. I could take the leap of faith before, but now . . .

I think again of the message in the sky, the summons to come home, and I feel sure that it's the person who saw through the chief from the beginning and who couldn't be convinced she was anything but evil.

Bella.

I need to get back to her.

Now.

When I'm back on the ship I swallow my fear and anger and go into my bathroom, with all the trinkets I charmed into it—makeup, jewelry, candles, and crystals. I was so excited to have all the things here that I could never afford growing up. It all seems so meaningless now, like a giant trick. And it was. My vision blurs, and I splash cold water over my cheeks. I take a long look at myself, waiting for my reflection to grab me, but she doesn't. Because she is me. I'm no longer the person grasping for her identity. I am who I am, for the good and the bad. And this me is not going to stand by for another second.

I shove the shell necklace under my shirt. With one last glance back at the room I have so loved, I creep down the hall, into the chief's quarters.

As I sneak through the chief's door, closing it behind me, I stop short. Hellion is trapped in an iron cage in the corner of the room, his beak taped shut. He hops around on the perch, wings beating against the bars.

"There you are," I say. "I knew you would never let something like that happen to Mal without a fight." I run over to him. "Sweet boy, I'm going to help you." Hoping the chief hasn't used magic to secure him, with a flourish of my hand, I animate the cage.

It comes to life, iron bars loose as spaghetti. A face forms on the door with a bulbous nose and a lock for a mouth.

"Let Hellion go," I say, checking behind me to make sure the door is still closed. "And hurry up. Don't waste my time."

"Right away, missus," he says, then makes a spitting noise as he sends the door flying open.

"Come on, boy," I say to Hellion. "You don't belong in there." Hellion looks at me for a second before hopping out and onto the chief's desk. "Don't bite me," I say, and when he nods, I pull off the tape. He immediately begins to chitter. "No, no! Quiet." I open a porthole window. "You're free. Go, my friend."

Once Hellion is gone and with no more time to waste, I move straight for the chief's apothecary shelf, between jars filled with mysterious herbs of every color and long white fingerlike shards of mushrooms, and pull the the chief's magic mirror from its spot.

"You're coming with me," I say to the mirror. "Where you can't do any more damage." Even holding it in my hand, even though it looks like any old mirror, I can't help but tremble. I am stealing this, the chief's most treasured possession, and I know better than anyone that there is no such thing as an inanimate object. There is only an object whose spirit is not activated, so what feels like dead wood and glass in my grasp is anything but. I can't even let myself imagine what would happen if the chief found me here.

I'd be *lucky* to walk the plank.

One thing is for certain: There's no turning back. I have to help the Vanished get home to their families, and I have to find a way to get all of us back to the Scar, once and for all.

I slip the mirror into my bag and turn around, only to find Hellion has returned, chittering, staring at something on the chief's desk.

"What are you doing? Do you have a death wish? You have to get out of here," I hiss. "Otherwise you're going to be crow stew, and you're far too pretty for that fate."

He cocks his head to the side, then peck peck pecks.

"Oh, fine!" I whisper.

I scan the desk. There's the chief's vase, filled with pink and black flowers, a tablet in a white case, and several folders that don't look overly interesting. Hellion looks at me and hops over to the picture she keeps in a silver frame. It's the photo of the chief and me standing together at the press conference after my parents and sister were murdered. I am a short six-year-old, with already-haunted eyes and a prim red dress. The chief is next to me in her officer's uniform. On the other side of me, Aunt Gia stands off-center with sunglasses on. She's been crying. I can tell because her nose is rosy, which always happens to her when she's sad.

My Seed mark twitches to life, writhing on my wrist. "What is it?" I murmur. "What does it mean?"

In answer, my Seed mark sends a stinging through my arm, and it yanks me to the door. I look back at Hellion and say, "I'm sorry about Mal. I'm going to fix it, I promise."

I stare into his wise eyes, and it's almost like I can hear him say, *There is no fixing this.*

"Good luck, friend," I say. "Now shoo!"

I jog down the hall to the magic room. Mercifully, no one is in there. I probably have another thirty seconds to get out of here.

Right on cue, I hear a muffled voice say, "Where is she?" It's James. I briefly consider bringing him with me, but I can't do that. Not now.

I scan the shelves of bottles, the pouches of pixie dust, the various

CITY OF MAGIC AND MONSTERS

wands, and the long table with supplies: glass bottles waiting to be filled, blue ribbons, and empty velvet pouches.

Before I lose my nerve, I stuff as many bottles of fully brewed magic as I can, along with two pouches of the dust, into my bag, cinching it closed.

I pray to all the fairy godmothers and all the magical creatures that have ever lived. I think of my mother, my mother's mother, and her mother before her.

Let me out of here.

The room trembles, an earthquake rippling over the carpet under my feet.

I picture myself in the Ever Garden, standing next to James, my hand in his, the power I felt. Light rushes into my body, filling my cells as a portal appears, a rip in the fabric of the air.

"Hurry," I hiss. "Take me home."

I am almost through when I see flapping wings as Hellion dives in and settles on my shoulders. He nips at my ear softly, telling me that there is no time to hang out and wait for what's next.

"Are you sure?" I say, and he gives me a single, irritated caw. "Okay, you asked for it. Hold on!"

We jump through the mirror.

We tip and slide and fall. We are upside down, tossed in spin-cycle turbulence.

I don't know where we're going.

I don't know if we'll land in one piece.

I don't know if I'm delivering us into the mouth of a monster. I only know we need to get out.

Black wings.

Digging talons.

ESTELLE LAURE

And then I'm spit right onto someone's floor.

Army-green carpeting softens the blow. My eyes are open, cheek flat against the ground. My body feels like it rejoins piece by piece, spine locking together until I am whole. I don't know where Hellion is.

"Mary Elizabeth?" I hear the voice. "Oh my gods, it's really her!" Footsteps pound, and two sets of knees hit the ground next to me. "Mary, are you okay?"

Wings flap overhead. "Bella?" I say, trying to get my bearings.

"Yes, it's me," she says.

"And me," another familiar voice says.

I pull myself to my elbows. I'm in a well-appointed living room with thin, stylish furniture and lamps made of crystal and glass. The hands pull me to my feet and draw me up.

I'm chest to chest with Lucas Attenborough, his every feature contorted with worry. "Are you okay?"

"We heard a noise and . . . oh, dragon's fire . . . you're here!" Bella says.

I push away from Lucas as a weight settles on my shoulders. Hellion squawks; then, after a moment, he calms down and goes quiet, observing everything around us. My heart twists dangerously as I think of Mally. I am still with her, still plummeting into the sea. I think she will be with me forever now. I will never be free.

"What's going on in there?" a voice shouts from another room, presumably the kitchen. "Are you all right?"

"Fine, Mom!" Lucas shouts, never taking his eyes off me. "An old friend dropped in for a visit." He quirks his mouth into a half smile.

"A friend?" Lucas's mother says. "What friend? I didn't hear anyone buzz."

"Mary," he says, "meet my mom, Maria." He spins me around so I'm face-to-face with a woman who is short, small, olive complected, with

113

CITY OF MAGIC AND MONSTERS

piercing, inquisitive eyes and a gold nose ring, her hair braided into a crown around her head. One arm is in a trench coat, and she has a cloth lunch box hanging from one wrist.

"Hello," I say as I extend my hand.

But Maria doesn't take it. Instead, she slaps her mouth, looking amongst us all. "The Red Queen," she whispers. "You're all over the news. Oh no . . . the Watch." She scurries to the windows and begins lowering the shades. "I have to go to work," she says when the apartment is in shadows. She looks between us worriedly as she flips on a lamp. "You need to get her out of here," she says to Lucas. She gives me an intense once-over. "Do you know you're the most wanted person in all of Monarch? You and the rest of them."

"I'm sure we are," I say, absorbing the fact that when we went to the school to get Morgie, we made ourselves the spokespeople for the chief's plan. If anyone were to need to be sacrificed, it would be one of us.

Another way to keep us in line.

"You made a complete spectacle of yourself," Bella says, folding her arms across her chest. "Now the whole town is back on villain duty."

Maria shoves her other arm into her trench coat and pulls a kerchief from the pocket, which she fastens over her head as she speaks. "My son tells me you are a nice person, so maybe we will meet some other day and we will have the chance to get to know one another, but for now, I need you to find a way out of here. I need my son to be safe."

"Okay," I say, "understood."

"You text me if anything comes up," she says to Lucas, giving his cheek a little squeeze.

She pats Bella's shoulder and bustles out, giving me one last suspicious glance and a shake of her head before she shuts the door behind her.

With the three of us alone, we grow silent, hovering near the apartment's front door. Hellion sits on my shoulder.

Just like that ... I am home again.

Now all I have to do is save the people I left behind.

PART II

TEN

The Spades had made a discovery, you see, and they knew
how dangerous the truth was: that if you went through a portal
to a new world, you could never return without destroying
the place you came from.

—*A People's History of the Scar*

LUCAS POURS FRESH CUPS OF TEA AND BELLA
takes her spot on the couch while I watch. After a few moments, I
sit across from them. I have questions about how they happen to be
in the same apartment, in the same room, but I sense it's going to
be my turn to answer questions, not to ask them. The scents of mint
and rosemary rising from the steaming cups immediately begin to
settle my stomach and give me the opportunity to get my bearings.

I am no longer on the *Mary Elizabeth*.

I'm on solid ground, at least for now.

I do not smell the sea air or hear the sounds of the Vanished rushing
around on deck. I cannot feel their anguish and confusion, or James's
heartbreak, or the chief's ire. There's an absence in the air here. The

CITY OF MAGIC AND MONSTERS

sparkle and glitter and possibility infused in every atom in Neverland—it's gone.

I can hardly stand to think of what must be happening on the ships now. If the chief has found out that I am gone and have taken her mirror—the only way out of Neverland—with me, I can only imagine how furious she must be. But she is outnumbered, and I don't think she could go toe to toe with James or Ursula and get anywhere at all. There's no way any of the Lost Boys would turn on them, so I try to let it go for now and pay attention to what's right in front of me.

Bella is keeping her distance. Now that she's gotten the initial embrace out of the way, I feel the hostility radiating off her.

The room is quiet and dark with the shades drawn, and the minutes stretch out. We all breathe together. After a snack of seeds and crackers, Hellion finds a spot at the top of a bookshelf and seems to be having complicated thoughts as he stares down at us.

The chief's mirror rests in my bag, warm and heavy. Even though it's only been minutes since I left the ship, it already feels like a dream of a dream. Somewhere, the chief must be realizing what's happening, that I have betrayed her, that I am gone and her mirror has gone with me, and that she is trapped.

"I can't believe you're actually here." Lucas's hands shake a little as he rests the cup on the table. "You look good."

I haven't known how to feel about Lucas since the night he knocked me out, took a syringe, and infected me with Wrong Magic, then released me and saved all of us. Before that day, I hated him. He was horrible to Legacy, smarmy and self-aggrandizing. But when he let me go so I could save my friends, everything changed. The moment he took the handcuffs off me and set me free, he chose what was right and good over his own father. His father who is now dead, killed in a car accident the day I went through the mirror.

"I would have called if I could," I say. "There are no phones in Neverland." I lift the teacup to my lips and consider how much truth to tell Lucas and Bella.

"Neverland?" he asks. "Isn't that what James and his dimwit worshippers used to call their house?"

"Hey, watch it, Lucas," I say. "Those are my—"

"Yes, okay." He puts his hands up defensively. "They are your friends. And James is your—"

"Heart," I say.

Lucas drops his chin. "Got it," he says. "I'm sorry."

"But yes, that's what James and the Lost Boys called their house, the house where they lived because they *had nowhere else to go*." I sit up a little taller. "Unlike you, they didn't have a golden apartment to live in." I look at both of them. "We had to give the new land a name," I say, finally. "Names are how you make a home."

Another tense silence meanders between us. I wait.

"Where is this . . . Neverland?" Bella asks primly, reaching down next to her spot on the couch and into her bag for a notebook. She pulls the attached black pen from its holder and clicks it, letting its point rest on a blank page, then looks up at me, scrunching her eyebrows together. She is incredibly adorable and as annoying as ever. "Where is it, exactly?"

There is no easy or sensible way to say this, because it makes exactly zero sense. But if Bella could send a message in the sky and somehow have it land with me, she can believe the truth. "I've been in Miracle Lake."

"In?" Bella asks.

"In," I confirm, taking another sip of warm liquid. "As in, on the other side of the water."

Lucas scoffs. "Oh, come on."

"Yeah, I figured you would say that," I say archly. "And still . . . it's true."

"And Jasmine?" Bella says, taking more notes. She doesn't look up when she says, "Is she all right?" The tension goes up several notches, especially when I show my confusion.

"What do you mean?" I let my cup clunk onto the table. "What would Jasmine have to do with anything?"

Bella stops scribbling and pushes her glasses back up the bridge of her nose, eyes moist. "You don't know?" She visibly blanches. "She's missing, along with Jack Saint and all the kids. I thought . . . I dearly hoped maybe she was with all of you."

"No," I say, trying to let her down easy. I can see how much my words have hurt her by the way she shrinks into her red mohair sweater. "I'm sorry, Bella. I don't know where she is." But the sense of dread is pooling at my feet like sludgy, oozing mud. I don't know if I am telling the truth. Maybe I *do* know where she is. Because the last thing Jasmine did before I left was publish an exposé about the chief, and I'll bet a fairy's wing Ito didn't like that one bit.

"But what now?" Bella says. "If she's not with you she could be anywhere, and I've followed every lead there is." She knits her brows. "There's no trace evidence, no sign of anyone having come or gone from the warehouse where she disappeared, and she left her phone. Nothing has been charged on her credit cards. I really, really thought you were the key."

"Belles," I say, searching for how to say what I need to say next.

122

She cocks her head to show me she's listening, but her expression is stern.

"I have to tell you something."

"Oh no," she says, reading the look on my face. "What?"

"There is *one* teeny possibility that Jasmine might be alive . . . well, almost alive."

"What does that mean?" She gets to her feet. "Spit it out."

"I don't know this for sure, so don't freak out, but she might be . . . at the bottom of the ocean." I sigh.

"As in, dead?" she asks, all hard edges, back straight as a broom.

"No."

"Then what are you talking about?"

"Keep calm, okay?"

"Tell me what you know and I'll decide whether to be calm or not."

"I only know that Ursula has a hideout in the sea, and she's doing something with the chief. It's some sort of enchantment and I think . . . I suspect Jasmine is being held there."

"The chief, eh?" Bella's voice goes cold. "Everyone here is claiming Chief Ito is dead. But she's not dead, is she?"

"No."

"And she is wicked, is she not?"

"I didn't think so until—" The words die in my throat. There's no point in defending my reasoning. I was willfully blind. That's all there is to it. "Yes. The short answer is yes."

"What is this deal between Ursula and the chief?" Bella asks.

"The chief's enemies . . . people she doesn't like . . . they get turned into some kind of algae and are being stored at Ursula's place at the bottom of the ocean."

"The bottom of the ocean that's inside Miracle Lake?" Lucas says, leaning back even farther in his chair, sliding his arms over the couch's headrest.

"Yes," I say. "As you must know, Ursula and all of us who got the Wrong Magic have different things we can do. I can portal and animate objects, even while I'm here. James can stop time and be very persuasive. The thing Ursula is best at is changing forms, for herself and others. Plus, she's got gills. So only she can have a garden under the sea. You know?"

They're both looking at me intensely.

"I think that's as close as I'm going to get to being able to explain it." I blow out a breath. "I don't know for sure, like I said, but I went there today—"

Bella opens her mouth, and I put up a hand to stop her. "I went there today, using magic Ursula gave me, and I am ninety-nine percent sure I saw Jack Saint."

"Okay," Lucas says. "This just got a lot more interesting."

"And so you think Jasmine is . . . what . . . *algae*?" Bella's voice goes up several octaves. "She's like those security guards that were on the news when you broke into the high school? Like Kyle's goons on the night of the Battle of Miracle Lake?" Bella says, and my heart breaks for her. "Shriveled to nothing? My beautiful friend is a . . . worm?"

"Listen," I say, desperate to give her hope. "If she is there, and that's a big if, anything that has been done by magic can be undone."

"Even death?" she asks.

"No," I say, thinking of Mally and now of Lucas's father, too. Death is death and there is no undoing it.

"The truth is, none of us are safe and none of us will be until the chief is brought to justice.

None of us says the obvious. That someone will have to answer for all of it, even if we can get everything restored. Those in cahoots with the chief will be wanted in connection with the kidnappings, and we went viral for doing it, and for turning government officials into worms. Either way, I'm likely to wind up in prison. It'll be back into cages for all of us. And what will happen to the Lost Boys and Smee? James? Urs?

I let out a burst of air. "I'm not saying we were right. I'm just saying we thought we were. So let's go. Let's go get them and figure out how to take down the chief, for real this time."

"Let's do it!" Bella says, getting to her feet. "Magic us over there with your portals."

"We can't do that," I say. "We have to be smart. Anything could happen. We have to know what we're doing. We're only going to get one shot against the chief. Much as you may not trust me right now, we're going to have to work together. And then, I promise, I will go get Jasmine."

"I'm sorry, no one is going to ask the obvious question? How could you be *in* Miracle Lake?" Lucas bursts. "People can't even get near that water. It equals instant death."

"Your dad was using the water to make the Wrong Magic. It just needs to be used the right way . . . harnessed, I guess. Miracle Lake is a mirror," I say. "Every mirror is a potential portal. That's just how it is. A mirror has a front side and whatever is through the looking glass, too. And what's on the other side of a mirror is anyone's guess. Well, on the other side of *that* mirror . . . is Neverland, a universe with water and mermaids. It's endless and vast. Not what you would expect. Not anything that makes sense to our logical minds."

"Mermaids?" Lucas says, arching a brow. "My dad had a mermaid's tail on his office wall. I never thought of it as belonging to a real . . . person."

"Ugh, Lucas," Bella says. "Gross."

CITY OF MAGIC AND MONSTERS

"I get where you're coming from," he says. "My dad was the worst. But I think he was trying to do the right thing at the very end. I do. And now it's up to me to finish what he started."

"Understood," Bella says. "Now, Mary, tell us more about Neverland."

"Okay." I search for the right words to describe what should be an impossibility. "Neverland is everything you need. Food can be magicked out of the air, there are ships, and dog poop disappears on command. But there's only water . . . a whole universe of it . . . and an occasional sandbank. At least, as far as we know. We haven't done much exploring. We dropped anchor where we landed. We've seen no sign of anyone else. There are flamingoes and it seems quiet, but under the sea, that's where everything is happening."

"Did you ever use the antidote?" Lucas asks.

I shake my head, not recovered enough to speak.

"Then I have one and you have one," Lucas says. "We can do something with that."

I cast my eyes toward him, then down to the floor. This was not the homecoming I was hoping for. I thought I would be marching through a portal to save my city from evil, and instead I'm steeped in shame for every poor choice I've made.

"Aw, Mary," he says. "What did you do?"

"I got rid of it. Threw it into the ocean."

"Why?" he asks. "Why would you ever do that?"

"Because," I say, "I wanted to prove I was one of them."

"And are you?" he asks, studying me.

That's not an easy question to answer. I'm not the person who first went through the mirror, that's for sure. For one thing, I look different. Even in these plain clothes, I'm not a normal teenager like I once was. My skin is smoother, hair longer and silkier and wavy, and I know from watching myself in the mirror that there is something heated in my eyes that didn't use to be there. Magic gives extra life, like plant food has been pumped deep into my soil, working its way through my roots.

That's the least of it. I feel different, too, like I've lived a lifetime at sea in a month, as though magic changed the experience of time itself. But when I think about life on the ship, about James and the Lost Boys who want to stay in Neverland forever, and Ursula who wants to live under the sea, and the Mad Hatter who is always by the chief's side, and the chief who is evil, and Mally who is dead, I also know I don't have a place with them.

"I am not," I say. "I am not one of them. Not anymore."

I think for a moment Lucas may start a fight with me, demand assurance that I'm on their side the way the chief would, but he only says, "Good."

"I thought I was doing the right thing. Until—" I am going to tell them about Mally walking the plank, but the words are stuffed in my throat. I shake my head. "Sorry," I say, shoving back the tears. "I'm not ready to talk about all of it yet."

Bella lifts her head. "Okay, but there are a few things we *have* to talk about. For instance, what is the plan?"

"Yeah," Lucas says. "I know you all haven't been sitting around over there for a month. What have you been doing?"

"Training the Vanished to use the magic that's their birthright, for one."

"Because . . ." Bella says, folding her arms across her chest. "You're going to attack Monarch."

"No!" I say. "*Attack* is not the right word."

She purses her lips at me.

"But also . . . yes," I admit. "If I hadn't left when I did, the Vanished would be portaling into Monarch tomorrow. All of them. And they'd be bringing magic, too."

"Magic?" Lucas says. "How?" Then he nods his head. "Ah . . . the chief."

"We've been stockpiling it. It's a very diluted form of Wrong Magic. A little blood, a dash of gold dust, and a drop of Miracle water," I say. "I stole as much of it as I could. I have it in here." I shake my bag, and it rattles. "But there's a lot more. One thing, though: The Vanished can't use their magic here without it. As soon as they're through the portal it goes away. There isn't enough magic in the air here. Only those of us who got the Wrong Magic can still function in Monarch. For us, without the antidote, anyway, there's no going back." Lucas looks away, guiltily.

"Does that mean the Vanished are alive?" Bella says. "I mean . . . all of them?"

A rush of annoyance heats my cheeks. "You're kidding, right? Of course they're alive," I say. "You really think we would hurt a bunch of kids?" As soon as the words escape my lips I feel their irony. After all, the chief did hurt a kid, and we are all responsible for letting it happen.

"I don't think *you* would," she says. "It's *her* I'm worried about. So, if I'm understanding, you have left two hundred or so children in Fantasyland—"

"Neverland," I say.

"In Neverland"—she corrects, consulting her notes—"with no way to get out?"

"Yes. But they're okay. At least for now. The chief is not going to destroy her own army. She'll just be out for my blood." I pause, letting this sink in. "I hope, anyway."

"We need to find out exactly what the chief is doing, what her actual plans are, because I'm not buying that all she wants is to give Legacy magic," Bella says. "I don't think she cares about Legacy at all."

"I promise she doesn't," Lucas says. "Let's remember she started out having a part in experimenting on them . . . you . . . in very unpleasant ways."

"So the endgame," Bella says, flipping her notebook shut and returning it to her bag, "is to figure out what *exactly* the chief is up to, then to bring her back here and return those kids to their families." She pauses. "And find a way to free the souls trapped in Ursula's garden. Agreed?"

"Agreed," Lucas says.

"Let's go," Bella says.

"I think the two of you should stay here. I can do this by myself," I say. "You heard your mother, Lucas. She wants you safe. And Bella. Think about your mom and your aunt."

Lucas gets to his feet. "Not going to happen. My dad started this mess. I have to finish it."

"I really thought I was going to be able to save the Scar," I say. "I thought I would be able to come back here and make everything better for everyone and you would all have magic, and everything would be the way it was before . . ."

"Before the Great Death," Bella says. "Before you lost your family."

"Yes," I say.

"Well, if you think I'm letting you do this alone after all we've been through together, you're mad." She turns to me, pointing her finger so close to my nose I can see its ridges. "It makes no sense that I love you so much. No sense at all."

CITY OF MAGIC AND MONSTERS

I straighten as Bella's words land like warm raindrops on my skin. I'm quiet inside, as though everything that's been sliding around the decks, unmoored in a hurricane, has finally found its proper place. "You love me?" I say.

In my peripheral vision, Lucas smirks.

"I—I—" Bella stammers, clutching herself even tighter.

"No, no. You said you love me."

"Oh gods, Mary, would you—" she says.

"You were worried about me because you *love* me," I insist.

"Ugh!" Bella leans against the wall next to me. "You're so annoying."

I belt out a laugh.

"I should kick your ass," she says, not looking at me.

"You just try it," I say, not looking at her.

"All right, team," Lucas says. "Are we all feeling better now? What's the first move?"

I head for the door, but Lucas goes to the window and checks behind the blinds. "Wait a minute. You're infamous, remember? You can't go out there."

"Actually," I say, "that is not a problem."

"Don't tell me you can make yourself invisible?" Lucas says.

"Not invisible. I can make us all very boring."

Bella makes a face. "What does that mean?"

"James taught me how to do it. All you have to do is think about how boring you are—"

"You?" Lucas says, letting the blinds snap shut. "Be serious."

"It works. But if you don't like that option, I can portal us."

"No, thank you," Bella says curtly. "We'll do your thing if we must . . . and in that case, I think it's very important that we begin by going to see someone who has been suffering as a result of your disappearance."

I spring up. "Aunt Gia!"

Sensing a change in the energy in the room, Hellion chitters and swoops onto my shoulder. Bella and Lucas eye him.

"Keep that thing under control," Lucas says, pointing to Hellion, who snaps like he's about to eat Lucas's finger.

"I wouldn't do that if I were you," I say. "He's in mourning."

Lucas watches Hellion carefully.

I turn to face them. "Now, give me your hands."

Bella lays her dry hand in mine, and Lucas squeezes the other. "Think of watching bad TV, brushing your teeth, reading a textbook about the intricacies of standing still." My fingers spark red light.

"You *are* different," Lucas whispers.

The light picks up and swirls around us, with more force and energy than it did when James and I were at the Ever Garden.

"Did it work?" Bella asks, an edge to her voice. "I don't see anything."

"I know you don't get this," I say, releasing them. "But that's not the kind of question you ask the Red Queen."

ELEVEN

All spells and charms must be opened and closed.
The circle must be complete.

—*A People's History of the Scar*

IF THE WATCH SEES US NOW, IT'LL BE LIKE WHEN James and I went to the Ever Garden. We'll only look like any other cluster of kids strolling down the street. As a first stop, we head to Aunt Gia's apartment. Maybe she has some answers about my abilities, answers that can only come from family.

As we step over a #LegacyLoyalty poster that's floating in city sidewalk muck, I ignore my own image, James's and Ursula's and Mally's profiles gathered behind me like a bouquet of bodega flowers.

Lucas and Bella flank me as we pass row after row of white SUVs, plus various men and women in gray who stand on the sidewalk. Bella hovers like she doesn't believe my charm will work. Hellion circles overhead, which gives me additional comfort. He would be squawking and flapping around if we were in imminent danger.

When we reach the apartment building at the edge of Miracle Lake, I glance around. Two members of the Watch are on patrol and a couple of news vans line the street, but when they merely nod at us, both Bella and Lucas finally seem to accept that my protection spell is real. The block is quiet, still, and Miracle Lake sits crystalline in the distance. The signs are there, proclaiming the water deadly, warning that to touch it would mean certain death.

My town. My lake.

My aunt.

The building's face is three stories of gray stone with long, rectangular windows and a blue wooden door. Like all the doors in the Scar, the doorknobs are huge and centered and made of metal, with a gargoyle sitting above the main ledge. I have passed underneath it thousands of times, but I have never felt nervous like I do now, like it's judging me, warning me that if I can ever get inside my apartment, my aunt Gia is going to kill me. I am all she has left in the world. She was thinking of accepting Jack Saint's offer to buy our apartment, had suggested maybe we could afford a little place on a beach somewhere, far away from here. Instead, I abandoned her, knowing she would never sell and leave town with me missing.

"I don't have my key," I say, raising my hand perpendicular to the door. "I'll portal us."

"You most certainly will not," Bella says as my fingers spark.

Lucas crosses his arms, gives Bella a pointed look, and says, "Well. You going to tell her?"

I rest my hand back at my side. "What is it?" I say, and Bella hesitates.

"I have a key. I . . . I've been staying here." She reaches into her pocket, sliding the key into the keyhole and turning it to the right, then swinging open the door. "Don't worry," Bella says as we step into the courtyard, closing the door behind us. "I couldn't replace you, especially not for your aunt. I was waiting for you, that's all. So was she. . . . We all were."

Waiting for me. Of course they were.

"So . . . let's go up?" I say, tightening my jaw against another tide of emotion as Hellion lands back on my shoulder.

"Yeah," Bella says. "Let's go see Auntie G."

When we reach the second-floor landing, Bella knocks, then lets herself in with a smaller key on her key ring. "G, I have a surprise for you!"

As she swings the door open to let Lucas and me in, I'm almost knocked over by the familiarity. All of Auntie Gia's things are just the way they were when I left, everything from the tatty old calico couch to the smell of lemon buttercream and vague top notes of honey and rosemary. I've missed all the plants, the coat stand, the TV with the lace hung over the top, and Auntie G's packing supplies: her pink ribbons and pinker bags and boxes and the plastic containers with lipsticks and skin creams that she uses for her job. I've missed the picture of my family, the four of us smiling by the river, sunglasses on; our dining room table with its four antique chairs; our windows looking out onto Miracle Lake, so close yet so far from everyone I left behind. The apartment draws a sharp contrast to the ship, the way everything was so fancy there, made of leather and metal and glass, every detail a reflection of the chief.

But the apartment also looks so much smaller than I remember it, back when I would come home from school and flop down at the table to do homework and wait for Gia to wake up so we could spend some time together. Now, I am a stranger here.

Gia emerges from her bedroom, and my heart splits in two.

Look what I have done to her.

My aunt has no makeup on, and her forehead glistens with lotion, her bangs held back with several rainbow barrettes. Her eyes are bloodshot, feet stuffed into velvet house slippers. It's like looking into a mirror that shows me myself in thirty years. She has also probably lost twenty pounds and looks too thin to be healthy.

"Oh, great ghost," she says, not missing a beat. "Oh, thank gods. My baby." She sweeps me into her arms so Hellion alights, and I'm smothered against her bony chest before I can even say hello. "I saw you on the news," she says into my hair. "It's been everywhere. The incident at school. At first I thought, that can't be my Mary. But it was." She hugs me even harder. "I was so glad to know you were alive. I knew you'd come back. I knew no matter how far you'd gone down the rabbit hole, you would return to me."

I don't know what to say. There's nothing *to* say. What's done is done. I can only try to fix it. Her skin feels warm and waxy, and she smells like butter and sugar and cinnamon and vanilla. That much hasn't changed, at least.

She strokes my hair, and we sway. I'll never be able to explain to her that I couldn't allow myself to think of her while I was gone. I couldn't dream of this moment. Maybe I was starting to warp, drunk on magic. Maybe Mally was the only one out of all of us who didn't completely lose herself.

Gia's attention shifts. "Bella, Lucas . . ." she says, still holding me close, remembering herself. "Thank you. Thanks to both of you,"

"Both?" I ask.

"They didn't tell you?" she says.

"Tell me what?"

"Well, we needed gold for the spell to bring you home. The Naturalists . . . we all did it together. And Lucas gave us his jewelry."

"A Rolex. It was nothing," he says.

"Lucas," I begin, but he stops me.

"Don't worry," he says, waving me off. "It's a drop in the bucket, just what I could filch from my dad's apartment before it all went into probate."

Bella continues into the apartment, stopping to hang her jacket on the rack where Hellion is sitting, scoping the room with eyes like black lava.

I take a moment to walk down the hall, looking at every detail: the striped wallpaper, the open bathroom door, Gia's bedroom . . . all the pictures of me, of my mother, of my sister. I push open the door to my bedroom, expecting that Bella has taken it over so much I won't recognize it anymore. But it's exactly how I left it. My satin sheets, my closet a sea of black.

"Come here, sweetheart," Gia calls, summoning me back into the living room.

For years after my family died, there was only Gia and me. The dining room table was our most special place. Here is where I told her the day I met Ursula. Here is where I told her I had fallen in love with James Bartholomew. And here is where I first experimented with the mirror when I missed James and Ursula so much, and begged it to tell me where they were.

Aunt Gia stuck with me through all of it, even when the Red Queen took over and I attacked her. So I know when she pats the chair next to hers that she's not asking me to sit down casually. She's asking me to explain what has happened.

"Yeah," I say. "Okay."

I share as much of the last month as I can, in as much detail as I can muster. I tell her about the magic, the ships, and about how nice the chief was at first, how she made all of us feel like we were doing something important.

"I'm sorry," I say, "that I wasn't here for you. I'm so sorry I made you worry."

"James and Ursula," she says after a moment. "How are they?"

"Ursula's got her own hideout," I say. "It's way at the bottom of the ocean. Actually, it's in a leviathan's skeleton. She has mantis shrimp guarding her house, and it's all full of treasure from shipwrecks."

"Oh goodness," Gia says. "That's so perfect for her. A place all her own."

"Yes," I say. "And James is completely obsessed with the ship and setting up the Lost Boys, making them feel like they're at home. Damien Salt and Wibbles are the chefs on board, and Smee sort of looks out for all the kids. I know it was terrible that I left the way I did, but it was fun for a while, at least for them. Like sleepaway camp . . . until it wasn't."

Gia clasps my hand and peers at me deeply. "And Mally Saint?" she says. "You haven't mentioned her. You know, her father is missing. After the dragon fiasco at Miracle, I thought maybe she would show up here and raze the city to the ground."

"I think she would have eventually . . . if she could." For the first time since I got here, I feel small and uncertain. "Mally's dead." Lucas and Bella, who have been sitting on the couch, whip their heads up so fast it's like they're on springs. Might as well tell them everything now. "She walked the plank, and the chief used magic to kill her. That's why he's here." I nod toward Hellion.

"I was afraid to ask," Bella mutters. "Now it's all making sense."

"The chief wanted me to cut off Mally's horns. That's how I knew she was really evil. It was like she was pushing me to see where my boundaries are." I squeeze Gia's hand. "She found them." Certainty roots me in place, and I strengthen again. "I never meant to hurt anyone and never wanted to see anyone harmed. I hope you can believe me."

No one says a word, and Aunt Gia stares at me like she's expecting me to disappear again any second. She's been worrying the sleeve of her robe but otherwise listening.

"I don't have time to waste, Gia. I left everyone stranded there, and I've got to get them back."

"Right," she says. "And then of course there's the whole issue of what happens when you open a portal to another world."

Gia says, swallowing. "This . . . this is very serious."

"I remember something . . . a family history, or a history of the Scar or something. Do you still have it?" I ask.

"Yes, that's right! That small-press book your grandfather had made just before he died."

"Books. The answers are always in books," Bella says.

"Hold on." Aunt Gia disappears into her room and comes back, holding a thin volume.

"This will help explain things," she says. "At least a little."

"I don't know if we have time to read a whole book," I say.

"Let me handle this," Bella says, and she gently pulls the book from Gia's grasp and disappears into the kitchen, where she hikes herself up onto the counter and begins flipping through the pages at a superhuman rate.

"It's too bad no one values the old ways," Gia says to Lucas. "If your dad had done a little research, looked into some history, he would have seen that nothing good was going to come of his efforts to tame and control magic. Everything has a beginning and an end." She smooths her robe and looks at me. "I made a mistake. I thought magic was gone and done for, though we Naturalists always knew it was more a case of abandonment than annihilation." She pauses. "I always wanted magic to come back, if for no other reason than it would have made my sister so happy."

"My mom," I say, loving the feel of the word on my tongue.

"Yes," she says. "She inherited portaling abilities. She was amazing, zipping here and there. It was our side of the family, the Spades, who had all the talent, and it was supposed to go down the female line. But I didn't have it. Never did. Not like my sister." She laughs, lost in the memory. "She used to *bloop* into the living room, pull my hair, and *bloop* out before I could retaliate. Our mother had portal skills as well. Portaling goes so far back in our lineage, it begins concurrently with the genesis of recorded history. And so, you can imagine how troubling it was for me that I inherited none of it."

"But you were a fashion icon!" I protest. "You were practically famous."

"Yes," she says, sitting down at the table again, "but I was never really a Spade like my sister. Everything was difficult for me, a push toward proving myself. I never married. I never had children. I stayed home and took care of our parents, and when they died, I was too busy to have any interest in relationships. When you and Mira were small, my sister and I got into a fight. We said awful things to each other, and we parted ways. Do you remember that?"

I shake my head.

"What happened to your parents came shortly after," she goes on. "I never got to tell my sister how proud I was of all her accomplishments, of her work in the field of feminist magical thinking. I was busy drowning my sorrows and my jealousies."

I'm bathed in pain, listening to Gia talk about my mom. I'll never really know who she was, other than the comforting presence I remember, almost in shadows now.

CITY OF MAGIC AND MONSTERS

"Anyway, I should have known you would have those abilities: floating, portaling, bringing things to life. After all, for you it didn't just come from one side. You had your father's gifts as well. A match made in magic heaven. And when magic came back and I saw you levitate, and when you started to act so strange, screaming threats at me, out all hours—well, I guess I had a fear response. I didn't want you to know about portals. I didn't want you to leave me, too. It's so silly to think you would want to turn away from magic."

"Aunt Gia—"

"No, no." She waves me off. "Just let me finish. I should have told you everything, let you make decisions for yourself."

"So now you're telling me because I messed it all up?"

"Not exactly." She leans forward, elbows on the table. "I always thought your parents' talents had something to do with their deaths. I don't know why. It doesn't make any sense. But you don't have to be magical to have an intuition, and mine always told me that portaling was dangerous business."

Bella catches my eye from the kitchen, and I can tell by the way her brows knit together that she agrees with Gia. Portaling is dangerous. After a moment, she wets her fingertip and continues flipping through the pages, one by one.

Gia shrugs. "I was mistaken, though. When they caught the killer and he confessed to the murders, I had to admit my intuition was wrong. Only now I realize I could have saved you some trouble if I had stopped you when I saw you playing with mirrors after the Battle at Miracle Lake, and especially after you levitated at the Naturalist meeting. It was obvious magic was back, after all, and who am I to try to control it?"

"That makes sense," I say.

140

"Somehow I thought if you could portal like your mother, you would die like her, too. I didn't want you to take risks."

"It's okay, Auntie G. I promise."

She sniffles. "I could have told you where you came from and what might happen. Knowledge is power. Of course it is. I hobbled you by not telling you everything. I thought I was keeping you safe. And now . . . well, what are you going to do?"

Bella hops down and brings the book over. Lays it in my lap. "I'm done," she says.

A People's History of the Scar, TrueHeart Press.

The book is covered in green velvet, and as soon as I touch it, my fingers vibrate and my Seed mark cranes toward it. I open the cover, and it creaks like old shipboards. Inside, written in black calligraphy, are the words *PROPERTY OF AARON HEART.*

My father.

"I took it from your parents' apartment," Gia says. "The police didn't consider it to be part of the crime scene. Your dad had it in his things. I always meant to give it to you, but as a memento, not an instructional textbook."

"Look here," Bella says, picking it back up and flipping to the middle.

"You read the whole book in ten minutes?"

"It's short. Also, I was speedreading champion of my college class all four years," she says. "Obviously."

"I didn't know that was a thing," I say.

"Stop nattering and look." Bella taps the page in front of me.

I scan the text as quickly as I can. The words jump out at me.

All spells and charms must be opened and closed.
The circle must be complete.

CITY OF MAGIC AND MONSTERS

"And here," Bella says, turning to another page she's holding with her index finger.

> *The universe is made up of doors. Portalers can find those doors and open them. Failure of a portaler to close the doors they have opened will cause tears in the fabric of reality. Enough tears in the same vicinity will cause the material to deteriorate.*

"Well, that's not me," I say. "I've just started being able to portal with regularity, and I don't do a very good job."

Bella peers over her glasses. "A portaler is someone who can create portals. It says here there used to be a ton of training around it. Back then, you'd have to learn to portal for years before you were allowed to do it with other people. There are all sorts of issues with time and space. If you make a portal and don't close it . . . chaos. Anyone who goes through it with you adds to the problem."

"How do you close a portal?"

"Beats me. Your dad didn't know. I think we need to find out though, because we're going to have to go back to Neverland and when we come back, with all those people . . ." She grimaces and shakes her head.

"There's going to be chaos." Lucas follows, grimly.

"Yeah," Bella says. "Unless you know the answer to that question, Gia, I think we're in trouble."

Gia's lips are a thin line. "I don't know. I've never known. It's not like the family was portaling through worlds. It was as forbidden as necromancy."

Bella takes off her glasses to rub her eyes. She looks like a completely different person without them, younger and more vulnerable. Purple

142

lines her bottom lids, and other signs of exhaustion are all over her. Her shoulders stoop.

The room wavers with tension.

We sit there for a few minutes, staring out the window at the bone-white sky. A siren wails, gets louder, and then fades off in the distance.

"We were good at that once," I say.

"At being cops?"

"Yeah, we would have been great ones. We would have helped people. If all this hadn't happened, we might have changed things another way."

"Ticktock." Lucas taps his bare wrist.

"I could maybe find a way to seal the portal between here and Neverland so there would be no more coming and going. Maybe there's a way to trap the chief there and bring the Vanished back."

"I don't know . . ." Bella says, wheels turning. "I don't know if that's enough to fix this."

"Well, what is, then?"

Lucas gets to his feet. "You heard what your aunt said. All this started when magic was forced back here. It doesn't want to be here. That's what's at the root of all of this. So that's it."

"What?" I say.

"Maybe instead of all of you having to stay in Neverland, we can send magic back to where it came from. Set it free. Let it go. Let *it* decide what it wants."

Understanding washes over me. "No more potions and shots and manipulations."

"Lucas Attenborough, you might be onto something!" Bella says.

"Well, that's a great idea," I say, "but how are we going to do that when we don't even know what's going on? I have a terrible feeling that this isn't about taking over city hall like she's been saying all this time. I think the chief has already done that. I'm betting whoever took over for Jack Saint is in her pocket."

Bella snaps her fingers. "You're right, Mary. Jack and the chief weren't exactly friends at the end there. I think this is all a big red herring."

The room goes quiet.

"Wait a minute," Bella says. "Didn't you tell me when you went to Reflections before you went through to the ship that you saw some man in there, buying a mirror for a lot of money?"

"A *lot* of money," I say, thinking of the elderly gentleman who asked for a special mirror and seemed very pleased to have it. He was dressed up like he was cosplaying Legacy. I had forgotten all about him.

"And was there anything special about the mirror?" Bella asks.

"Not that I could see."

Bella purses her lips. "And who owns Reflections?"

"The chief," I cough out.

"Let's go!" Lucas says, jumping to his feet.

Gia rises from the table and hugs me like she's sure I won't be back then leans back, searching my eyes. "Whatever you do, don't forget who you are and where you're from. And I love you, okay?"

"I love you, too," I say as Hellion hops aboard my shoulder. "Everybody ready to be boring?"

"Boring as they come," Bella says.

"Boring as cold oatmeal," Lucas adds.

"Okay." I glance at Gia and say, "I can't go back to who I was. And I'm sorry for that. But I am not sorry for who I am now." My fingers zap and fizz with red light. It forms a hoop around the three of us before settling back down. "Bye, Auntie G," I say.

"You three look completely different," she says, voice dazed.

I kiss her on the cheek, and her hand goes to the spot. "Be careful," she adds. "Please, please be careful."

We run down the stairs out the courtyard door, and onto the street.

"You know," Bella says after the three of us have walked a couple of blocks, Hellion on my shoulder. "It just has to be said. I told you the chief was evil. I told you not to chase after your friends. I. Told. You."

Instead of infuriating me, it fills me with the warmth of familiarity. "Feel better now?"

Bella purses her lips and rolls her eyes. "No. But it's a start."

TWELVE

There are as many worlds as there are mirrors. They are found
at the intersection between magic and destiny.

—*A People's History of the Scar*

THE SIGN FOR REFLECTIONS SHIMMERS SILVER ON
glass. Cars are parked all along the sidewalk. Boarded-up storefronts checker the block, which, not so long ago, was quaint, with
its cobblestone street and decorative flowers.

COME INSIDE AND MEET YOURSELF, a sandwich board reads in curlicue
handwriting.

I wonder if Rose Red, the chief's niece, still works in the store. She's
no fan of her aunt's. I was able to get that much out of her when I was
there the last time. Maybe that could be useful now.

The three of us walk through the door, Hellion on my shoulder, and
past the unmanned front desk. The door to the back is open and I'm
hopeful Rose Red is here, but I want to look around before I call out. In
the store, the air is crisp and cool. It looks the same as it did the last time
I was here, still divided into two rooms. In the front is a display of glass
cleaners, special cloths, and oil for maintaining the wooden frames. The

146

mirrors in that room are new, standard, and there are multiples of each. Mirrors to hang on the backs of doors: full-length, entryway, and even a few bathroom-cabinet styles.

"Oh my wand," Bella says. "This place is amazing."

We slip to the back, where I found the mirror that took me to Neverland. Each mirror is unique, every spare inch of space covered, and those too big or cumbersome to hang lean up against each other along the wall like canvases in an artist's studio, all shapes, all colors: rectangles, flowers, diamonds; blue, red, raw wood. There are mirrors to hold, simple, with hardly any edges, and ones with huge, gilded frames.

"Look at that," Bella says.

We appear in all of them. Infinite Lucases, Bellas, and Mary Elizabeths, crow perched on her arm.

It smells of dirt and hard work and traces of sulfur.

"Someone's been practicing magic in here," I whisper. "I'm sure of it."

Hellion chitters his agreement.

Before Lucas or Bella can respond, a voice calls out, "Anyone here?"

Rose Red, I mouth. I quickly swirl light around us and remove the spell. I need her to know who we are so she'll talk to us. Although there is a real possibility she's not too happy with me.

She pops around the corner, wearing a leather skirt and pink top. "Sorry I didn't see you. I was in the back. There's so much to do in this place." She smiles a customer-service smile but then does a double take. I watch now as the full impact of who I am settles over her. "It's you."

She doesn't threaten to call the Watch, and she doesn't look like she's going to attack or anything. I take this as a sign that it's safe to proceed. "Hi, Rose," I say. "These are my friends, Lucas and Bella, and this is Hellion."

Rose Red crosses her arms over her chest, all her politeness dropped away, but stops short when Hellion leans forward. "Oh, don't you *hi* me," she says. "You lied to me about your name and stole a very valuable mirror, and don't even try to tell me you didn't, because I know you did."

"You said those mirrors were all spoken for," I remind her. "I was only guessing that there was something more to them."

"Well, I lied, but it's none of your business that I lied, because you are a *thief*."

"I was only a thief out of necessity," I say.

She shakes her head. "What, do you think I'm stupid? I know who you are . . . Your *Majesty*. The words sound much less complimentary, oozing sarcasm, than they did coming from the mermaids. And anyway, my aunt told me you were coming here and not to bug you if you snooped."

This stops me.

She furrows her brow, scrunches her mouth into a knot. "I was disappointed you did exactly what she said you were going to, though. When you came in here that day, I really thought we were going to be friends. I thought, 'Gosh, Rosie, the world is on fire, but there are still worthwhile people in it. Isn't that excellent news?'"

"Listen," Lucas says, cutting her off. "I don't mean to be rude or devastate your belief in the relative goodness of humans, with or without magic, but we don't have much time."

"Oh," she says with added interest.

"Someone I knew died today, and I'm trying to fix it," I say.

"I'm sorry. I've lost people." She considers me for a moment, then says, "When you figure out how to fix death, let me know."

"Yeah," I say, thinking of Mally. "I guess I can't. But I want to make sure it doesn't happen to anyone else. You can help me with that."

Months ago, I saw the Red Queen in a bathroom mirror at Wonderland. It had a sticker from this place on it. So I came to find the store. That's when I met Rose Red for the first time. Then my Seed mark started going all batty and I was drawn over to a mirror, which, yes, I stole. I used that mirror to get onto the ship.

"I'm sorry about your friend," Rose Red says now, watching me carefully.

Bella pushes past me and goes right up to Rose, who looks her up and down, assessing her. "We need your help," Bella says.

"Yeah?" Rose says. "What kind of help?"

"We need to know why random people from uptown who have nothing to do with magic would pay a ridiculous amount of money for a mirror."

"Are they portaling?" Bella asks.

"Why would you say that?" Rose says, straightening an oval-shaped mirror and trying very hard not to look at us. Bella and I exchange a subtle nod of agreement about her shifty behavior.

"Come on," Lucas says. "We need to know. It could be really really dangerous. Don't let Ito scare you."

"Ito?" Rose Red's face drops, going ashen. "Oh no. You turned on Aunt Charlene," she whispers to me. "Which means you're in big trouble." She goes to the front door and holds it open. "I'm sorry, but you're going to have to leave."

"Don't worry," Bella says, blocking Rose Red's path to the other room. "We'll protect you."

"That's what we're trying to do," I add. "Protect everyone."

Rose Red bites her lower lip and shakes her head. "Look," she says to me. "I don't know who you think you're messing with. She's always watching."

"With what?" I reach into my bag and pull out the small rectangle. "This mirror?"

"Great ghost," she says. "You took it?"

"Yes," Bella says. "She did. So you can talk to us. Your aunt can't do anything to you. Not now."

"We know she's a monster," Lucas adds when Rose Red doesn't speak. "We also know we can stop her. But we need your help. Because if we can't do this now, we may never get another chance."

Rose Red lets this sink in, then strides outside and pulls in the sandwich board.

Bella, Lucas, and I all look at each other. I slide the mirror back into the bag. Bella gives me a small nod as Rose Red shuts the door, spins the OPEN sign to CLOSED, and locks the deadbolt.

"I'm wondering," Bella says, after a beat, "why are you working here? You don't like your aunt, right? So . . . why?"

Rose Red blows her bangs upward. "Ugh, okay. It was actually a huge mistake. A few months ago, Aunt Charlene came over to my apartment. She told me she was going to help me get out of that place. All I had to do was let her give me some magic, which I wanted anyway, obviously. She said she had it in a shot, and that it would be safe and everything. She said she had perfected it. She needed someone to make these mirrors. She couldn't do it herself."

"You?" I say. "You're making the mirrors magic?"

"Yeah," she says. "That's basically all I do around here. It's kind of exhausting."

"And you had the Wrong Magic?" Bella says, looking her up and down. "But you look totally normal."

"So do I," I say.

"The later iterations of the formula worked better," Lucas confirms. "Mary's proof of that."

"Thanks," I say.

"Yeah." Rose Red shrugs. "Anyway, it wasn't like I had never done it before. The Great Death happened when I was eight. I already knew how my magic worked. So did my aunt. I did it by accident when I was little and she was over for family dinner. There we were, after spaghetti and meatballs. Aunt Charlene was fighting with my mom . . . I don't remember over what. It was smoky and loud, and no one was paying attention to me. My sister, Snow, was cleaning up, I think. I used to love to play with Aunt Charlene's makeup, and I had her little handheld mirror, you know, for putting on lipstick? I was thinking about how much I wished it would lead to some other place, that I could escape somewhere, and all of a sudden, the mirror came to life."

"Like, animated?" I ask, thinking of my own abilities.

"No," she says. "Like, it got bigger. And there was something on the other side. Aunt Charlene came over a lot after that. We played all the time, changing mirrors." She sighs. "It was fun, and I definitely liked the attention. Everyone always preferred my sister to me. But for a while it seemed like life was good. My aunt brought me presents and stuff and made me feel special."

"She'll do that," I say, and Lucas pats my back.

"Anyway, the magic left, and that was that."

"Until she and my dad brought it back," Lucas says.

"And now, I'm just here," Rose says. "I collect and magic the special-order mirrors that are in the back room. She pays me really well." Rose shrugs again. "I don't know . . . she's sneaky and all full of secrets, but she was okay . . . until she started threatening me, telling me she was going

CITY OF MAGIC AND MONSTERS

to hurt Snow if I ever tried to quit, telling me she was going to be back and we'd be shutting this place down to go to some warehouse and start production, that she could see everything I did and was watching me." She grimaces. "It's like I'm going to be a prisoner or something, like my whole life is just going to be this."

"Is there anything else you can tell us?" Bella asks. "Anything at all that might help us?"

A siren wails by outside, but otherwise the place is completely quiet. "If I tell you what I know, you'll stop her?" Rose asks.

I put a hand on Rose's shoulder. "You are going to be okay, we promise. We're going to take care of this. You won't be a prisoner anymore. We just need information. That's all."

She leads us into the back room again. "All I know," she says, "is these have been charmed, and the guys from uptown who wouldn't know magic if it sat on their heads . . . they pay a lot of money to have one of these mirrors so they can spy on people, listen in on conversations, that sort of thing. Way easier than planting bugs. See? She got them hooked on that magic." She takes her phone from her pocket and pulls up a note. She scrolls and scrolls. "I've been keeping a record of messages. They keep calling—saying they're waiting for the next thing. I think she has something even bigger planned, or at least that's how it seemed, but then she dropped communication."

"What did she say the last time you saw her?" I ask, a strange feeling coming over me.

"She told me there was going to be another phase to all this, that I should keep on going like I had been but she was going to be ramping it up. And then, like I said, she threatened me. She actually told me if I messed up, she could turn me into *seaweed*." She shivers. "I got the feeling she meant it, too. Totally freaked me out."

The chief was so excited when I finally portaled without any additional magic. It was like it was her own personal victory, more than just about me and what I had accomplished. She was thrilled. Somehow, all this is connected.

"Thanks," Bella says. "You've been really helpful. I'd suggest you get yourself as far away from here as possible. Find somewhere safe and lay low for a bit."

"Lady," Rose says, slumping against the counter. "Nowhere is safe from my aunt. So you better do a good job."

Bella grabs Lucas and me each by a sleeve and points us toward the door.

"Do your charm thing, Mary. We have to go." She unlocks the door as I quickly spin the light around us again.

"Boring," I say.

"Boring as reading a toaster manual," Lucas says.

"Boring as the patriarchy," Bella says, closing her eyes. "Hurry, Mary."

When the charm is done, she says, "We need to go talk to Dally Star. He's been in business with the chief for years. He must know more about all this than he's admitted to in the past. We have to find out what she *really* wants to do with those mirrors."

"Bye, Rose," I say. "Thank you. You've done the right thing."

Rose Red gives us a sad smile. "Yeah," she says. "Watch your backs."

THIRTEEN

To put a finer point on it, the universe is made up of doors. Portalers can, in rare cases, find those doors and open them. Failure of a portaler to close the doors they have opened will cause tears in the fabric of reality. Enough tears in the same vicinity will cause the material to deteriorate.

—A People's History of the Scar

WONDERLAND HAS HAD A FACELIFT. THE POOL tables are gone, replaced with foosball. Gone, too, is the croquet game I loved so much. Instead, there's Skee-Ball, and air hockey where the stage used to be. The lighting in the main bar is yellow and bright, and the music is basic and bland. We pass by the table Lucas and his friends used to pay for so they could sit and watch all the Legacy from on high.

We scan behind the bar, and there's no sign of Dally. Lucas roams while Bella and I search nooks and crannies for anywhere he might have gone. The walls have been repainted a flat white. TVs are all over the place, displaying tonight's football game.

"Where's Dally?" Bella asks.

"I don't know." I quickly undo the charm.

"Bigger question: What happened in here? Dally's changing with the times," Lucas says.

Dally Star comes shooting into the room.

"That was fast," Lucas murmurs.

Dally's hair is in a bouffant, and he has his pink bedazzled glasses, white suit, thin mustache, same as always. He smiles, showing all his teeth, and opens his arms wide.

"That *was* you," he squeals. "I was looking on the monitors and I saw you come in, and I thought, I think that's Mary Elizabeth, but I couldn't tell. And then I put on these glasses and saw you clear as a sunny day." He taps at them. "They're charmed, you know. When I'm wearing them I can see *everything*. It is! And look! You've got Hellion!" Even from where I stand, I can smell the tangy lime of his cologne. "Pray tell, what does this mean, young miss?" He fans the air in Hellion's direction. Hellion is unamused and snaps a warning with his beak. "Okay! All right!" Dally says, uneasily. "Not in the mood, are we?" Dally peels his eyes from Hellion and pastes on another big smile. "And you're with Lucas Attenborough?"

Lucas nods.

"Never thought I'd see the day!" He giggles nervously. "And hello, Bella, and welcome in!" He leans in. "Although, perhaps this isn't the *best* choice?"

"Best choice?"

"Well, yes, all things considered I mean. What with the events at Monarch High, the serial kidnappings, etc. If I can see through your magic, one must assume I am not the only one." He pauses before scooping me into a hug. "Even though you've done a silly thing coming in here, it's amazing to see you, really. I mean that sincerely. You look wonderful, absolutely wonderful." He locks arms with me and steers me out of the main room as Bella and Lucas follow behind. "But you can't be seen in here. Oh no no no no. It won't do at all.

"Dally, we have to talk to you. We're not going to leave until we do."

He assesses me, drops the smile and sighs loudly, finally speaking in a much more subdued tone. "Fine. Let's go in my office."

"Bella—"

"She can't come," he snaps. "And neither can he."

Hellion flaps his wings and caws loudly like he's my deranged feathered muscle.

"Oh no," he says, clamping his hands over his own mouth like I'm sure he wants to do to Hellion. "No . . . please. Shhhh."

"Dally," I say, "you know I'm not going anywhere without them."

"Oh, fine," he says, giving them another long look. "Come on." He leads us upstairs, behind the bar, through a door, and down a hall I never knew was here. The third door on the right has a heart in the middle of it, and Dally guides us into a large room filled with trinkets, surrounded on all sides with books from floor to ceiling.

"Wow," Bella says. "Look at all the books!"

"Well, yes," Dally says, "I'm somewhat of a collector. People, books, baubles . . . you know how it is."

"Bella heaven," I say.

Something moves on the other side of the room, and I see a large wooden cage filled with white bunnies.

"Rabbits?" Bella says.

"White rabbits," Dally says, crossing the room to reach through the slats so he can pet one of the little fluffs. He pulls out the tiniest marshmallow of a bunny and comes over to us. "You want one? The mama just had babies, and I'm overrun with them." He plops it into

Lucas's arms, where it immediately curls into a ball and closes its eyes. Dally watches fondly as Lucas strokes the bunny's ears. "Don't you ever wish you were an animal instead of a person? It would be so much easier, don't you think?"

"Not really," Bella says. "They only want to pull each other apart. Nothing is more brutal than nature."

"Not my babies. They're protected with me and live the best lives ever." Dally coos at them for a minute before turning his attention back to us.

Hellion natters and eyes the bunny in Lucas's arms.

"No," I say to him. "Bunnies are not snacks."

"Something to drink? To eat?" Dally says from the corner, where he's set an electric kettle to boil.

I shake my head. "No tea today, thanks, Dally."

Dally comes over to me and holds my hand. "Everyone is looking for you. There are people out there, people who would love to snatch you up and serve you on a platter to the powers that be. Have I taught you nothing all these years? I'm disappointed. Duck and weave. Always duck and weave."

"Yeah, Dally. I'm trying." He looks at me so tenderly, I think he might actually care.

"We're here for answers. We need to know about your business dealings with the chief," Lucas says.

Dally blanches.

"And we need to know about the portals." Bella keeps her eyes trained on him. He's trying to maintain composure, but his face is pinched with nerves. Bella hesitates just for a second, and I can see the wheels turning in real time. "And we also need to know how Mary figures into this. Mary"—she hesitates—"and her family."

Dally looks like he's about to pass out.

"Oh no. Oh boy," he says. "I don't know about this one here"—he indicates Bella—"but I've always loved you, Mary. Please don't make me open up old wounds. I feel bad enough already. I loved your parents, too, and was so sorry, so sorry for what happened to them."

Bella eyes me sharply. Her gambit for information we didn't know Dally had has struck a nerve. And it is my job to press into it, to get us what we need. Good thing I don't need any more of a push than the mention of my parents. In fact, I have to hold myself back

"What does this have to do with my parents? You knew them?" I edge in on him. "You never told me that."

"Of course I knew them," he says. "The Scar is smaller than it seems."

"Why didn't you . . . How could you not tell me?"

Dally is searching for his words, tripping over them as he glances from me to Hellion and back. "I didn't know it was something I should have to say to you. I know everyone in town. I grew up here. We're the same age. I assumed you were aware."

I'm struggling to take all this in. "I never knew how old you were. I never made that connection."

"Yes well, young people don't think beyond themselves much, do they?"

So much is lost in small talk, and that's really all Dally and I have ever done. Gossip. A little verbal sparring. And all this time, he knew my family. They were all young together.

"Wait . . ."

"I was so silly back then," he says. "We were in our twenties, I remember when Charlene Ito approached me about working together, and I was so taken by her. I thought I was so fancy, that I was going to be one of the elites. In fact, I remember your parents and Ito getting into an argument a few weeks before they died." He points toward the window that looks down over the pathway that leads to the lake. "It was right out there. This place was dilapidated back then. It wasn't Wonderland yet. Only a dream in my head." He sighs, glumly. "And I suppose it isn't Wonderland anymore, either. I don't know what it is." He shakes his head. "I'm just trying to survive, but it's not pretty these days. The Magicalists were right after all. Magic was real, and it was coming back. It never really left us, did it? It was just running underneath our feet, underground. But that doesn't matter now, no, it doesn't."

He keeps going, but I can't hear what he's saying anymore. I'm stuck on what he said about my parents and the chief.

"Were my parents and the chief friends?" I say.

Dally shrugs. "Back in the old days, we all knew Charlene. She didn't have any real magic. She was Legacy, but she had to use spellcraft to do anything. Even then, she needed help." He winces. "Don't tell her I said this, but she just really wasn't very good at it. It was problematic, especially as we all started to get older, find our specialties. She sort of floated along." Given what Dally has said, it makes sense then that she would want to be in Neverland where magic is everywhere, and that she would be interested in experimenting to find a way to control it.

"You saw them arguing and you have no idea why?" I fold my arms across my chest, stuck on this point. I know there's something more to all this. I can feel it in my bones. My parents are connected to everything that is happening right now. It's eerie, as though they are standing next to me, hands on my back, pushing me to find the truth. "Come on, Dally. You're the most curious person I know."

Dally hesitates, just a second too long.

"What?" I press. "Tell me."

CITY OF MAGIC AND MONSTERS

"No, nothing. It's just . . . your parents were wonderful. Your mother was the most talented portaler around. She was a Spade, after all. But they didn't have a lot of friends. They were a little—"

"What?"

"Internal or something," he finishes. "Private. Mysterious. Not always friendly."

"Wow," Lucas says. "Apple. Tree."

Lucas might mean it as a dig, but it lands as mysterious and lovely that I might be anything like my mother.

"I don't know what they were fighting about," Dally says. "Honest. I have no idea."

"Dally—"

"I don't know! I swear!" he insists. "I wasn't going to go meddling with the three of them. They could have been arguing over the weather." He shrugs. "And Charlene has become something else since then. I thought it was a good move to go into business with her. I wanted to take care of my mom and make something of myself after the Great Death. We were all left with nothing, you understand? But when I asked her about the argument, because I did, eventually, she told me it was none of my business and to shut my mouth about it. She didn't want her name besmirched by my paranoia. It made sense at the time. She had a lot to lose. Her career was on the rise."

In my training as a detective, they told us to let silence be. People talk when you give them the rope to hang themselves. Bella and I exchange glances and let Dally stew while Lucas looks between us, waiting for someone to say something.

"And then, later, she came to me with a proposition," Dally says, finally. "I wanted magic back so badly." He wrings his hands, then

160

raises his delicate fingers to his temples. In here, away from the club, his outfit, the makeup, the glitter . . . it all looks so cheap. "You don't understand what it was like for us when the Great Death happened. Out of nowhere, magic, the thing all our lives revolved around . . . was just gone. It was devastating. There were a few who thought it simplified life, but for most of us, the light went out. We were abandoned. Exiled. And so, every building, every street corner, and everyone left in the Scar was still there, but in a way we all disappeared without it. Magic *is* us, don't you see?"

"What was the deal?" Bella asks. "What was the deal you made with the chief?"

"Your dad," Dally says to Lucas, "and Charlene, and my old friend Jack Saint, offered to buy me Wonderland, to let me have it as long as I let them do what they needed to do." Dally tries to take my hand, but I pull it away. "You won't love me anymore if I say, and that would hurt, Mary. That would *hurt*."

"Tell us," I insist.

Dally looks between us all. "They needed funding. Jack Saint was broke. Chief Ito—because she *was* the chief by then—was broke. They were both in debt. The plan was to tap into the vein of magic that lives underground here. The Narrows had found out about it and started drilling. But it wouldn't work. Every time they got near it, it bounced them back. Killed a few people, too."

"Poisonous," Bella says. "To them . . ."

"They were about to give up when the chief and the mayor realized there might be one more thing to try," Dally says.

"Kyle Attenborough," I say, tracking.

"Your dad," Dally says to Lucas. "The richest man in Monarch."

CITY OF MAGIC AND MONSTERS

"Unlimited resources for experimentation," Bella murmurs. "All the Legacy you could ever need, right at the end of your personal fingertips."

"But why would Jack Saint ever let anyone experiment on his daughter?"

"Oh, yes . . . that," Dally says. "He and the chief had a disagreement about how to proceed. Jack didn't want Kyle and her experimenting on actual children, though I'm sure she did it anyway. Who else was going to keep quiet about it? They'd be more easily controlled. But Jack wanted to find another way. She punished him by making Mally the first."

It hits me all at once, all the pieces coming together. I can tell Bella is having the same thought. "The case," she says.

"What?" Lucas says. "What are you talking about?"

"Mally got into trouble. She assaulted Flora and Fauna and Merryweather. The case against her was open. The chief must have lured her somewhere to talk about it under the guise of police work," I say. "And then bam, she dosed her."

"You," Bella says to Lucas. "What was your part in all this?"

"No," Lucas says. "Nope. I didn't have anything to do with Mally. She just appeared at the lab one day. She already had horns. They must have been keeping her somewhere else first. I swear. I didn't do it!"

"Okay," Bella says. "So what *did* you do?"

Lucas takes the bunny back to the cage and reluctantly places it gently inside the hutch. "My dad told me to start making friends with Legacy kids," Lucas says. "I tried, but it wasn't working, not at first. I went to Ursula. I knew she was always wheeling and dealing, and I told her I could show her something else, something that would change her life. She brought James, and I guess the rest is history."

They didn't bring me, though. Why would they? I was a detective.

"Jack Saint would never have allowed Mally to be a part of this. That's why he came to the station that day, when he was trying to find her. He must have known the chief had something to do with her disappearance. Of course!" Bella says.

"But he couldn't make a scene," I say. "Because then the whole business plan would fall apart. And what if he was wrong? What if something totally unrelated had happened to Mal? He probably couldn't even imagine the chief would be so brazen as to steal his kid out from under him. I'm guessing the chief wanted Mally's magic since she doesn't really have her own. But Mally's always been . . ."

"Hard to pin down," Lucas says.

"To say the least," Bella agrees.

We have all seen Mally lose her temper. Back at school she could clear the hallway with a glare, and her magic was powerful. Too powerful for the chief's liking.

Hellion nips at my ear, chittering excitedly.

"Meanwhile, knowing how much the children of the Scar wanted magic back, all the chief had to do was give Legacy kids a taste of magic and they'd follow her like a siren." Bella folds her arms over her chest, turning her attention to Dally once more. "How could you do that to your own people?"

"I didn't know it was going to be like this, that they would hurt people, create monsters. What else was there?" Dally says. "You were little when we lost magic. You don't know what it was like, how painful, how . . . sad. I thought I could look the other way if it would bring magic back. Those paranoid numbskulls in Midcity were only ever going to stand in our way. They loved it that we weren't special anymore. But," Dally says, "the chief needed you, Mary. I don't know for sure, of course, because I have never been her confidant, but I suspect she wanted your portaling abilities." He hesitates. "You can portal, can't you? Like your mother?"

I nod. "I'm learning."

Dally squeezes my forearm. "You have it all inside of you. That makes you very important to the chief. You understand?"

"Not really," I say. "But I'm getting there."

I do understand one thing though. Months ago, when Jack first came into the police station, looking for Mally, that was the beginning of Bella and me having our strings pulled like brainless puppets.

"Bella," I whisper.

"Shut up." She clutches my arm. "Don't say it."

"I just wanted my club, my place, a little money, maybe? Maybe a spot for music and art? A little sparkle, a little magic." Dally mutters, talking mostly to himself, lost in his own memories, and hopefully a bit of guilt, too, for the part he played. Though I'm in no position to judge. After all, I watched Mally die and I did nothing. The desire to protect ourselves is stronger than we think and we only find out when we're tested.

"She knew you would never go of your own volition. She had to tease you into it," Bella says. "To give you something to chew on. Steps to follow. Things to discover. The case," Bella says. "Mally's disappearance. The Mad Hatter. None of that was real. It was all a setup."

"Well, almost," Dally says. "The magic did warp the kids. I was sorry about that. I don't think anyone thought that would happen. And they did have to be quarantined. And your father, Lucas, had decided the whole operation had to be shut down. That night, if you hadn't gone into the lab, Mary, Ursula, and Mally and James wouldn't have made it out alive."

"And meanwhile, your friends knew you wouldn't go with them unless you thought it was the right thing, Mary. They used your own heart against you, to lure you," Bella says. "And the chief needed you. She would not just be in charge of everything in our world, she could travel into other worlds and take control there, too, with no consequences."

Dally continues to ramble under his breath, circling, muttering on faintly, circling the room, and all I can think is that everything that happened to me—getting the internship, getting the case to find Mally, being kidnapped, the Battle at Miracle Lake, searching for James and Ursula—it was all just a ploy to get me in deeper and deeper.

I pushed down every gut instinct I had from the very beginning. Nothing lined up. Or maybe it lined up too well.

Hellion squeezes my shoulder, nickering, and rubs his beak against my cheek.

"I'm sorry, Mary," Dally says. "So very sorry. I can't. I can't do this. She'll be coming for me. I have to leave. I'm sorry. I have to go!" He's been inching his way toward the door and now he throws it open and runs out. We hear his footsteps pattering down the hall toward the street outside.

"Wait!" Bella yells.

I run, ready to follow him, but Bella pulls me back. "You can't go out there. You need the charm!"

I rip my arm away from her, and she falls into Lucas. He loses his footing and falls back into the bookcase, knocking a book from its place on the shelf. As it tips forward, the bookcase swings opens Behind it is a gaping black hole. A secret passage.

Lucas looks up at me from the floor. Bella squints into the dark.

"Look at you, Lucas," she says. "Good job."

I pull Lucas to standing. "I guess . . . I mean, I hope I've done one thing right."

"You have," I say. "You're doing it, okay? You're making up for the past. And I'm glad you're here."

He blushes, wipes the imaginary dirt from his pants and clears his throat.

"Are you two ready?" Bella says, looking between us.

"Let's go," I say.

And then we walk behind the bookcase, into a rabbit hole, into the darkness of whatever it is that Dally has really been hiding. Because I don't know much, but I know Dally didn't tell us the whole truth.

FOURTEEN

But the people of Monarch forgot that magic was a miracle,
and they became greedy. Their desire for money trumped
everything. And so, magic left them. They cried. They mourned.
The portals disappeared and the people suffered, and the
Legacy forgot who they were.

—*A People's History of the Scar*

"I'VE HEARD OF SECRET PASSAGEWAYS BEHIND
bookcases, but this is a whole new level," Lucas says.

"The answer is always in books," Bella says. "Haven't you learned that
by now?"

We're in a passageway made of packed dirt. It stinks of mold and
mud, and I can hear the skitter of creatures unsettled by our appearance,
see their shadows running for cover. In the distance in one direction,
it is black and opaque, and down the other way, a dim yellow light
flickers.

"Where are we?" Lucas whispers.

"Have you ever picked up a rock that's been undisturbed for a long
time?" Bella says.

"Once, when my mother made me go camping," Lucas says with a shudder.

"Well, I think this is the bottom of the rock."

"That," I say, pointing at the light, "is Wonderland. Probably the storeroom or something." I turn toward the darkness. "That's where we want to go."

"This is a little bit exciting, don't you think? I'm starting to feel like my old self!"

Bella is in perky mode, and I couldn't be happier. At least something good is coming out of all this.

When I stand straight, my hair brushes ceiling. Hellion has hopped off and is bouncing down the passageway ahead of us. Lucas has to stay bent at the waist.

My fingers turn red, then send out sparkles that ripple and illuminate Bella and Lucas and Hellion. I search for signs of danger, threats, bigger bodies or guards or hexes, but there's nothing. The air is dead except for the crackle coming off my finger. "Keep an eye out for anything jumpy," I say.

"Oh, great," Lucas says. "Just wonderful."

Bella and Lucas are hesitant, careful as they make their way, and after a few steps I can't take it anymore. I detach myself from them and march forward. If I'm going to walk into a wall of darkness, I might as well make it quick.

"My dad told me he thought the chief had gone rogue," Lucas says. He seems to be comforting himself with his words, talking about his dad, keeping his mind busy so it doesn't scare him with images of lurking monsters. Or maybe I'm reading into his monologue. Maybe he is just talking and none of it means anything. "That's part of why he tried to detach himself from the whole thing. That didn't work the way he had planned, though. Not at all. And look at this place. Disgusting."

"Worried about your Italian leather again, Lucas?" I tease. Back before he was whatever version of himself he is now, he once got in a fight with Stone Wallace and made some crack about his shoes. I have to remind him how terrible he was, at least every once in a while. And anyway, it eases some of the tension, at least for the moment.

As I reach the end of the hall, I see what looks like a giant round metal bolt. Hellion flaps up and hurls himself against the metal. "Stop it!" I say. "Let me figure this out."

Hellion glares at me like I'm wasting precious time. "We just got here!"

"How are we going to open this?" Bella asks.

I flick my wrist, and for the first time ever, a portal immediately appears, like it was in my hand all along and I threw it into midair. It circles and crackles until it's large enough to be a doorway to the other side.

"The government is so lucky you're not a psychopath like they said," Lucas whispers. "You'd be terrifying."

"Come on," I say.

We all climb through to the other side. We're in a cement room with high ceilings. Flickering neon lights hang down and hurt my eyes as they strain to adjust. Shelves line the walls all around us, filled with bottles of liquid and powders, gear that is all too familiar to me from my time in the magic room at Neverland. The buzz of machinery comes from somewhere. "Close the portal!" Bella calls, meandering out of view. "Remember what the book said!"

I follow my instincts, willing my mother's ghost to help me. I whip my hand around, gather the energy, and make a fist. With a flash and a sizzling sound, the portal disappears. I'm expecting some

CITY OF MAGIC AND MONSTERS

acknowledgment, but Bella is nowhere and Lucas is already occupied. Oh well. I'll just have to be impressed with myself.

"What is it?" I say as I go over to where Lucas has begun picking through a box on one of the shelves.

He pulls out a pair of shackles that clink heavily against each other. Underneath are piles of zip ties and a bottle of formaldehyde, along with a series of soft cloths. "Why would anyone need all of this, unless . . ."

"Unless," I echo, easily imagining all the wicked uses for the items in the box.

"MARY!" Bella's voice carries, ghostlike, from the next room. I didn't even see her go in there.

Lucas and I both run toward the sound, but then stop short.

The room connected to the one we came in through is dingy and sparse and there are big cases of some kind, with shadows everywhere.

I start to make light from my fingers again, but Bella says, "Hey, look what I found!"

Lights come on one by one, creaking to life, and my mouth drops open.

All around us are cases, about eight feet high by four feet wide. And inside each of them is a monster, far worse than anything we have seen up until now. They float in some kind of liquid that doesn't dampen their clothes. In one, a wraithlike demon with orange eyes, a human body, and a round head stares dead into the center of the room. Goose bumps climb my skin as I walk from tank to tank, like a guest at a museum of horrors.

I pass a woman with rows of shark teeth; a boy with knives for hands who has cuts all over his own body, mouth pulled into a pained grin; a girl in gauze with the haunted, gaunt face of a ghost; conjoined twins with hands coming from everywhere.

"What happened to them?" I say, unable to avert my gaze. My Seed mark judders to life, sending off a warning.

"Look at this guy." Lucas leans in to read the label at the bottom of one glass tank. "Chernobog," he reads. "What's a chernobog?"

I shrug.

"Well, whatever he is, it's next-level. They look like serial killers."

"Or victims." I look up at the twins, bobbing silently in the viscous liquid. "So what are they doing here? Are they just going to be left here like this forever?"

"I doubt it," Bella says. "Whether this is another secret testing facility for the Wrong Magic, or something the chief was working on that Kyle didn't even know about, it can't be an accident that it's still here. She's too smart, too careful. If these were failed experiments like Ursula and James, they'd either be destroyed, or with her in Neverland. But since they're not, that means she's got something else in mind. These monsters aren't evidence that needs covering up. They're part of her plan."

"Agreed," Lucas says. "I have a bad feeling about this."

"Me too," I say.

"Why would she need them?" Bella says. "Think. Think."

"I don't know," I say. "But can you imagine these things descending on Monarch?"

Bella blanches. "Oh no."

"Yeah," Lucas says. "I guess it's not a very complicated plan."

"It's her backup army." A new level of discomfort unwinds in the pit of my stomach, the knowledge that I could animate these things in a heartbeat. A person shouldn't have that much power, should they?

Bella puts her hands on her hips. "Okay, so what do we do now?"

We take one last look around. "I'm going to portal," I say to Bella. "I think we shouldn't waste any time . . . you know . . . walking."

"Yeah," Bella says, rubbing at her shoulders like she has a chill. "Let's go."

"Go where?" I say.

"My house," Lucas says. "I'll explain when we get there."

"You're going to be mad I didn't show you this when you were here earlier," Lucas says after we've landed safely in his living room. "But before you turn into a two-headed monster like those creepy twins, I didn't know it meant anything until now."

We're back in his apartment, still shaken by everything we've seen, and it feels normal and good to have Hellion on my shoulder again.

When he swings the door to his bedroom open, Bella gasps.

"My thoughts exactly," I say.

There's no TV, no video game console. There *is* an expensive-looking walnut wardrobe. His bed is too big for the room, his sheets too valuable for a home in the Scar. A desk sits to one side, with only a closed laptop to decorate its surface.

And all around us, on every wall, are mirrors upon mirrors upon mirrors. Small ones, long ones, handheld and decorative.

"Where did you get all these?" I ask.

"My father's estate is in probate, but I'm not stupid. Like I told you before, I got a few things out of the apartment before the Monarch PD wrapped it in red tape."

"A *few* things?" Bella says.

"These were in your apartment?" I say, brushing past her.

Lucas nods.

"Why did you go for the mirrors?" Bella asks.

"I had heard my dad talking about them. Only whispers, but he brought these home before the Battle at Miracle Lake. I don't know . . . I thought they might be important." He goes over to the wardrobe and frees up the bottom panel. He retrieves several manila folders. "I grabbed this stuff, too."

"You're hiding things from the police?" Bella says. "That is highly illegal." She swishes over to him and pats him on the shoulder. "Also, good job."

"The night he died, my dad gave them to me. I just . . . didn't volunteer to give them back. They've been sitting in there this whole time. I . . . I haven't been able to look at them. Just seeing his handwriting . . ."

"May I?" Bella says.

Lucas hands them over.

"You okay?" I ask him.

"Sure I am," he says. "And if I'm not, it doesn't matter, does it? This is where we are." Lucas closes the wardrobe with a click.

"You take this one." Bella hands him a thin folder. "You take this, Mary, and I'll look through this big one."

Her file is labeled *MIRRORS*, while mine is labeled *INFINITY*. She flips hers open, still standing in the middle of the room.

"What are we looking for?" Lucas asks, sitting down at his desk chair and laying the file open flat. "We already know my dad was trying to tame magic."

"I don't know," Bella says. "I just have a feeling there's something here."

I flip open my file and see ovals and squares with squiggly lines behind them. The writing is fastidious and small, and urgent. It's hard to read, and I try to focus.

CITY OF MAGIC AND MONSTERS

"My dad was old-school," Lucas says. "Never caught up to computers. He loved science and money, but he didn't trust technology."

"Probably because he was an evil overlord," I murmur, then remember myself. No matter what Kyle Attenborough did, and no matter how his actions are still having rippling effects, he was Lucas's father. "I'm sorry."

Lucas grimaces. "It's okay. You're not wrong. It just sucks. But maybe he can do some good now, you know? Maybe. I'm glad he went this route and gave me all this. I think he was probably right it would have been stolen if I hadn't gotten to it."

Bella takes out her phone. "May I?"

"Sure," Lucas says, and instantly Bella is snapping pictures, adding to her mounting collection of evidence.

When she's done, her face disappears into the file. She pulls off her glasses and cleans them on her jacket, then slides them back over her ears.

I search and search, everything complicated and difficult to understand, the words running together before it all starts to make a sick kind of sense. "Great ghost!"

"Wait, what?" Bella looks up, startled.

"What is it?" Lucas echoes.

"Am I reading this right? This says there are infinite portals."

She peers over my shoulder, then hands me a page and shows me a diagram of a mirror with lines shooting off in every direction. "Every time they try to fix a problem they create a thousand new ones."

"Or in this case, infinity new ones?" I say.

"What are you guys talking about?" Lucas says, suddenly on high alert.

"This is a copy of a memo between your dad and the chief," I say. "It was an email, but it must have gotten wiped at some point, because . . ."

"What does it say?" Lucas asks.

"It says that when he started screwing around with Miracle Lake, he figured out that was the source of magic. But it was more than that, which he found out from all his researchers."

"Like Mary said, it led to another land," Lucas says.

Bella squeals and sits up. "Look at this! These are field notes from one of his scientists. She found that if you add Miracle water to mirrors along with Legacy blood, they can get to every world that has ever existed anywhere. Abandoned worlds, imagined worlds, everywhere, all over."

My head spins. I never thought to ask the chief about where we were, where the ships were anchored. I just assumed it was some bit of her magic, that she had invented a safe place for us. But she didn't invent it. She *found* it. Of course she did. Otherwise that whole world, all the mermaids, Ursula's house under the sea . . . none of it would have existed.

And it looks like it's one of many.

"They decided they were going to start mining, building, doing what humans do," Bella says. "They were going to portal through mirrors, awarding people land for the right price. This is so much worse than what Rose was talking about." She looks up. "Lucas, why didn't you give us these before?"

"Honestly," he says, "I never even looked at it. I . . . I haven't been ready."

"It was Jack Saint, your dad, and the chief," I said, redirecting our attention to the folders. Time is ticking away and the pressure to get back to Neverland is mounting inside me. Whatever is happening there cannot be good. "I bet the chief didn't like sharing or reporting to anyone."

"They were going to sell mirror memberships," Bella says correctly interpreting my intensity. "Grant access to worlds where magic was more accessible. They were going to try to control . . . everything. Every world that has ever existed or ever will, anywhere."

Seconds tick by as I absorb what this means, trying to get my mind to catch up.

"Well," Lucas says, finally, "no one can accuse my dad of thinking small."

"What the hell happened when they tried the mirror magic?" I ask.

Bella grudgingly hands me the folder. "Bad things," she says. "Even if a portal is opened and then closed, as it should be, it still has a permanent effect. Like that book said, every time someone goes through a mirror to a whole other world, it creates a tiny tear in the fabric of our reality that never really heals all the way."

"So . . ." Lucas rubs his temples.

"The flamingo," I murmur.

"Flamingo?" Bella says.

"Yes," I say. "When we went to Monarch High to get Morgie, a flamingo came along with us. It wasn't anywhere near the mirror we came through. It must have found some sort of opening."

"All those people coming and going through different portals. It would eventually shred reality." Bella pushes her glasses up the bridge of her nose. "I'm sorry, Mary, but even what you and your friends have been doing, coming and going between here and Neverland . . . it hasn't been safe. As a portaler, your involvement has managed to limit the damage. Without you, this would all be . . . catastrophic."

The room goes silent.

That's why the chief needed me. I would be helping her put infinite worlds at risk, and meanwhile it would all have been for money. When she asked me to cut off Mally's horns, she wanted me to prove, once and for all, that I would do anything for her, anything she asked of me.

She was banking on the fact that I was still the sad little girl who lost her family at six years old and only wanted someone to love her for everything she was. She didn't realize I don't need her for that. Because I love the little girl I was. I will hold her close.

I will keep her safe.

"The chief was warned what would happen if she kept playing with dimensions." Bella holds a paper under my nose, too close for me to read. "It's right here in this memo. Jack Saint, your dad, and the chief all met. They suspected if they started messing with portals it was going to cause major issues. Dammit!" Bella's lip trembles. "It says here they were told there could be huge consequences. They were warned by those scientists. They knew—"

"The Fall. They caused the Fall." As soon as I say it, I know I'm right. "Magic had enough of being pushed around. They were misusing it, hurting Legacy, trying to get rich. They were going to invade. Magic knew they would have destroyed everything, every world. So all those people died because of them. They didn't even care. They just went right back to what they were doing, only now they had Miracle Lake, sitting right there like an open wound."

And all the while, Jack Saint, Kyle Attenborough, and the chief . . . they knew it could happen. They knew, and they didn't stop it. No wonder Jack Saint was so dismayed and determined to keep Mally close. The night of the Fall, when the Wand disappeared, he had accidentally killed his wife.

I look to Lucas for confirmation.

"It makes sense," he says. "The vein of magic that runs through the Scar went right under that building. That's where they were digging. They knew there were risks."

"Magic got angry," I say.

"This is why I couldn't look at all this stuff. I knew I would find evidence. You know. Evidence that my dad was a bad person. Evidence that would mean he didn't just have a random accident in the Scar. That someone accordioned his car on purpose. He'd outlived his usefulness to the chief."

Bella slaps down the file. "We've got to get those kids, make them understand that the chief is evil."

"They'll never give up magic," I say, thinking of all their games, all the magic they get to play with, how much they wanted to be on the ship forever.

"We have to make them," Bella says. "We have to convince them they need to come back here in peace."

Hellion swoops into the room and takes his place on my shoulder. He squawks and nips at my ear. "Hellion is right," I say.

"You and the bird are speaking some secret language now?" Bella asks, twisting her mouth into a smirk.

"Mally sent him to me," I snap, satisfied as the smugness slides off her face. "You wouldn't understand."

"Okay then," Bella says, leaning toward Hellion, who makes a low whistling noise I take to mean that Bella should keep her distance, which she does. She straightens and plants her hands on her hips. "What's next, dear bird?"

"We know what's next." I pause, and Bella and Lucas look at me blankly. "I have to go back to the ships."

"Absolutely not," Bella says. "Why would you do that? It's too dangerous."

I give Bella's arm a reassuring pat. "Thank you for looking out for me. I'm grateful. But I have to fix this, and now. Because do you think the chief is just sitting around over there?"

"No," Lucas says. "The answer is no."

"If we leave all those kids there, who knows what will happen? She'll find a way to march on Monarch with the Vanished, whether she has her mirror or not. She'll unleash those horrible monsters on the city. We know what she knows now, what she can do. It might take her longer but she'll figure it out. But if I go back, there's a chance I can at least get the kids home safely. Maybe I can even stop her." I face them both. "You did your jobs," I say. "You helped bring me to my senses. You called me to the Scar. We figured out what is really going on. Now, I need to undo the damage I've done. I need to bring the Vanished home, and bring the chief to justice."

Bella scowls, and Lucas strokes his jaw thoughtfully.

Bella places the file on Lucas's desk. "Then I'm going, too."

"Me too," Lucas says, deciding.

"Not a chance," I return. "You've done enough, Bella, and Lucas, you can't use magic."

"But we're a trio, and I need to see it through to the end, no matter what," Lucas says.

Bella harrumphs. "And clearly, you need me for common sense."

They're not going to take no for an answer. I open the bag I've been carrying with me and pull out a couple of vials of magic. "Show me your wrist, Bella."

"What? Why?"

Before she can say anything else, I take the needle from my bag, poke her finger with it, collect the blood, and wipe it on her mark. I pour the magic over the top. She watches with obvious fascination as the mixture sizzles and swirls.

"Wicked," Lucas says when it begins to rise, then dives under her skin and comes crackling as blue light from her fingertips.

She grins. "That doesn't feel terrible. What will it do?"

"It's different for everyone. Let's see what happens."

Bella drags her eyes away from the light. "Are you going to?" Bella asks. "Take the magic potion?"

"I don't need it," I say. "Lucas, stick close to Bella. And both of you, remember, there's magic everywhere in that place."

"What's the plan, then?" Bella says, pushing her glasses back up the bridge of her nose. "Should we discuss?"

"Please," I say, spinning the air in front of me until a hole opens. "Who needs a plan?"

"Mary," Bella begins, and I pull her in for a hug.

"Mmmph," she says.

Lucas joins in, looping us both into an embrace. "I hope this is okay," he says, voice muffled by my hair. "I just want to be part of the gang."

This sends Bella and me into fits of hysterics far more ridiculous than his joke deserves. But it buries the tension for a few seconds, and for that we are all grateful.

"Okay," I say as the sphere widens in front of us, revealing the black and white of the chief's quarters. If we're going to do this, we might as well go in full throttle. "You ready?"

I look at my friends. My only real ones, I guess. Lucas with one curl falling over his forehead and his black, determined eyes; Bella, lips pressed together, jaw tight, hands in fists. I hope this will not be the last time we're all together like this. One thing is for sure: Whatever happens when we cross into Neverland is going to change everything.

"Ready," Bella says.

"Yeah, me too," Lucas says. "If I die, lie about me. Tell everyone I was great."

I take each of their hands in mine. "You are great," I say. "Both of you."

"You're great, too, Mary," Lucas says. "You're both the best, giving a guy like me a second chance."

"We are going to be fine," Bella says. "I know we will. Our story does not end with that woman winning."

"No," I say, "it doesn't. If I go down, I'm taking her with me."

I'm about to be in for the fight of my life, and I am ready for it.

FIFTEEN

But magic was not truly gone. It was only underground.

—*A People's History of the Scar*

WE LAND EXACTLY WHERE I WANTED US TO. ONLY we're not in the chief's empty quarters, as I'd hoped. Instead, the moment our feet touch the floor and the room comes into focus with its leather and metal, I hear the sound of people clambering to their feet. Hellion, who is on my shoulder, swoops out the window, cawing loudly.

"Everyone at attention." I hear the chief say it but I don't see her.

"Aw, Mare," Smee says. "Why'd you have to go and do this?"

We're surrounded, knives pointing at us from all sides. I slowly lift my eyes to see who is holding them. It's my friends, of course. Ursula and James and Smee and Hat.

"Welcome back," the chief says, emerging from the corner in her good old white suit.

Bella's breathing goes shallow beside me as I scan the faces of the people holding the weapons against us.

James is brandishing the bejeweled dagger, eyes storming and red.

"You brought the A team," I say, relieved that at least Hellion is out of harm's way. I tear my gaze from James.

"More than I can say for you," the chief says, mouth curling into a self-satisfied smirk.

In the chief's hand, she holds something golden and glowing that rocks and rolls in a glass ampoule.

The antidote.

"But . . . how?" I ask. "I threw that into the ocean."

"I found it," Ursula says. "Flotsam and Jetsam were playing catch with it when I went down . . . after."

"After the chief killed Mally," I say.

"It's sad all around, honeybunch," Urs says. "Choices were made. By everyone." Ursula scowls at Bella and Lucas. "I'll never understand why you tossed us aside like rotten seaweed out of loyalty to these two losers."

"I think it's time to make decisions based on something besides loyalty, don't you?" I say.

"I don't know what you're talking about," Ursula says. "Loyalty's all we've got."

"No, it's not. We've got love, too. Love for each other, for the Scar, love for the greater good."

"I don't want love," Ursula says, "I want power." But I see a glimmer of something else slithering underneath her words. Something like hesitation.

"Hmmm," the chief says, an index finger tapping her chin. "So interesting. The greater good, you say?" She clucks. "No no no. Don't try to paint what you did as honorable or selfless. You and Mally got power hungry. You were conspiring to overthrow me, take all our magic, and turn the Scar over to Jack Saint so he and his friends

CITY OF MAGIC AND MONSTERS

from Uptown could run us into the grave, or worse, keep us alive and use us at will."

I consider making something up, but why bother? The time for lies and tricks is over. She knows as well as I do that Jack Saint is missing, along with Jasmine and dragon knows who else. I might as well tell the truth.

"When I saw what life was like here, when you showed me your home at the bottom of the sea." I turn to James. "And when I saw you, on this ship, living the life you always wanted with these boys. And even you, Hat, getting to do tricks with your knives and snacking on magical bakes . . . well . . . I understood I could never use the antidote on you. I could never force you to give up magic. But we're all just being used." I turn back to the chief. "And maybe Mally *was* conspiring against you. But that's only because she saw through you."

"We know about the mirrors," Bella adds quietly. "We know you only want to take over Monarch so you can control magic, in this world and every single other one you can get your hands on." She pauses. "We found your basement warehouse full of creatures and we've seen the paperwork, warning you about messing with portals into other worlds. You have no more secrets."

"We know exactly who you are," I say. "You're just a sad old woman who was never very good at magic. Your friends were dazzling, special. But you were nothing but ordinary. Even then, you needed potions and spells to do anything. Now you need the Vanished, you need me, and Ursula, and James, and even Mally. I see right through you. Because without all this—all of us—you're nothing."

A grin spreads across the chief's face like oil surfacing through pavement cracks. I don't know how I could ever have thought she was anything but evil. She sidles over to her apothecary and pulls a crystal decanter off the wall. She takes her time, pouring it into a

184

chalice, then drinks the potion. It's many times the dose we give the Vanished. James and Urs glance at each other as purple light crackles around her.

"You've been snooping and meddling and questioning long enough," she says, placing the chalice back on the shelf. She folds her arms across her chest. "You're a disappointment. A real disappointment. Almost as much of a whiner as your stupid little parents and your pathetic sister." She pauses as her words land, one by one. Maybe something happened during that conversation that made her angry enough to hurt them. "Oh yes," she says. "They cried and begged for their lives. Your name was the last word to come out of your mother's mouth. Drivel. All that moaning. All that . . . *weeping*."

The room is dead silent. No one moves.

But the chief doesn't realize what she's done. She doesn't realize what she's said.

She's surrounded by children who have lost their parents.

And she has just admitted to killing mine. I should have put it together when Dally mentioned witnessing an argument between my parents and the chief.

I want to rip her head off her shoulders.

Scarcely giving me a glance, she says, "Shrivel her," like she's ordering a ham sandwich.

Ursula looks between us, tentacles dancing across the floor underneath her. "Chief?"

"Prove yourself, right now."

"You said we were going to talk some sense into her. You said taking her by force was the only way—"

"James," she says. "Do something useful with that hook, would you? Take care of this problem for me?"

James, upset with me as he is, takes a step back. "Sorry, Chief," he says.

"Hat?" she says. "Dear Caleb?"

Hat looks between us for a beat, before slowly placing his hatchets into his holster. "Not this time," he says.

The chief settles on each one of them as though memorizing their faces for later. "Suit yourselves. I don't need you anyway. I have two hundred others, waiting for instructions." She raises her hand, palm facing outward, lip curling. "Let's have one of our little chats, shall we?" she says, as light flies from her hand and hits me in the chest, knocking the breath out of me.

Bella and Lucas both lunge to support me and fear ripples through the room. "Don't help," I wheeze, as I drop to my knees.

"You are going to do exactly what I tell you from now on," she says, inching in toward me, step by step. My friends are shadows behind her. "And if you don't, I will kill every single person you love, one by one, in front of you, and you will have to live with that, knowing forever that it is *your* fault. Because you know what your problem is by now, don't you? All. That. Love." She leans into me. "Stop fighting me. You cannot win."

My mouth drops open, then snaps shut. The room grows larger around me. This is because I am shrinking, as though I've been held together by thread and am now being pulled apart at the seams, stitch by aching stitch. The room is fading into shades of purple and the chief is fading, too, as are James and Ursula and Hat and Smee and the boys. I can't feel Lucas against my back. I don't know where Bella is.

I cannot breathe.

I don't have lungs.

Soon, I will be nothing.

She is turning me into nothing, a nothing she can keep in a basement somewhere, in a cage.

I can't think.

I.

Can't.

Think.

I hear a growl, fierce and low.

A caw. The flapping of wings.

The world disappears into rainbow light.

The last thing to go is sound.

And then there is nothing.

I'm holding the chief's hand at the press conference after my parents died, and the chief is swearing to the large crowd that she's going to catch whoever did it. She's saying I am a child of the Scar and to her that means something, that criminals who prey on the newly vulnerable Legacy, those without magic, will not be tolerated. She will be the Scar's protector. This will become her platform.

Lights flash all around us.

I look up at her, and she is tall and majestic and so beautiful, and her hand is cool and reassuring in mine. I believe in her. I believe she will protect me. I believe she is a friend. I will stand by her side again, again when my family is buried, again when the men are caught, again in court. Over and over, we are together, the chief and me.

This is how her power starts to grow. When she finds the men who slaughtered my family, she catapults into the public eye. Soon she is with celebrities on the weekends, eating in fancy restaurants Uptown. Then she is named lieutenant, captain, and finally chief of police.

I stop hearing from her.

CITY OF MAGIC AND MONSTERS

I try for a normal life in the Scar, living with Auntie G.

I go to school, I come home from school.

One day in first grade, a girl named Ursula gives me an orange marker, and we become friends. Years later, I meet a boy whose father has been jailed and whose mother will follow closely behind. Magic is dead but life is still magical, and we have the perfect weather, the mood clouds above us, and the Ever Garden to remind us of who we are.

Most days I don't think about the chief, but when I imagine my life in the future, I feel my fate will be intertwined with hers. I want to put criminals away like her. I want to hold a little girl's hand and make her feel safe, standing at the mouth of a cruel world. Or better yet, I want to put monsters behind bars before they even have the chance to put the girl there on that stage.

One day, I get an invitation for an internship. If I am accepted, it will be the first time I'll see the chief in many years. I apply, hands sweating from nerves, wanting everything to be perfect. I'm not a person who is capable of perfect.

I draw outside the lines.

My feelings are huge and overwhelming.

I walk into doorways and scream into pillows.

I miss my family, every day, always. I want my father, my mother, my sister. I want them back. I want to undo what has been done. I want it more than anything.

I get that internship. It will be months before the chief calls me into her office, acknowledges all we've meant to each other, pulls me in on a case in the Scar.

About a missing teen girl named Mally Saint.

And I can't wait to show her what I can do. I can't wait to prove that she was right about me all along.

ESTELLE LAURE

* * *

I come back to consciousness, my guts twisting snakes, pain shooting through my limbs. I try to scramble to my feet, but my body is battered and weak and I fall back down. It's shadowed and dark. No lights are on. The ship is ghostly. I don't know where my friends went. I don't know where the chief went, either. It is far too quiet.

As I scan the floor, trying to see, I find spatters of blood on the carpet. I feel my own body for cuts, but I can't find any. That's not my blood. My chest hurts. My arms feel bruised. My neck is cranked at a painful angle.

I look up.

Lucas is to my side, and Bella is over me, her mouth open in an O as though she's in the middle of giving me frantic information, but I can't hear her words.

As the room comes into clearer focus, I use the table to pull myself up. I'm not totally solid on my feet, but I can stand.

My sluggish brain begins to put together the pieces of what's happening. I grab my dagger out of my boot, heaving. James must have frozen time.

"Come on, boy," I hear. "Please."

I stumble to the door, where the voice is coming from. I pull it back to find James crouched down, Barnacle beside him, on his side, motionless. James looks up at me, eyes wet with tears. I sink down beside him.

"What happened? How long have I been out?" I ask.

"I don't know. A few minutes maybe?" He seems confused and lost. "Hellion and Barnacle attacked the chief. They were defending you, and then . . . I don't know . . . she did something to him. I think he might be dead. Hellion flew out. He got away." He lets out a guttural sob. "Gods, she was evil all along. I thought she was the one adult we could trust. But it turns out there's no such thing. She hurt my dog. He never did anything to anyone. He's such a good boy."

"Where is she?" I say. "Where did she go?"

But he can't hear me. He's too steeped in grief. "The chief struck Barnacle down and I—I couldn't bear it," he moans. "I didn't know what was happening to you. I didn't know if Barnacle was okay." James stares at Barnacle, whose eyes are open and fixed. "When time starts again . . . what if he's—"

"He's not. He can't be. Don't even think it." I stand up again and offer him my hand. "Come on," I say. "Find the fire in your belly. We have to finish this."

"Be okay, boy," he says, stroking Barnacle's ear. "Please." He accepts my hand, eyes flashing red. "I always knew I'd follow you to my death. I just didn't think it would be this soon."

"We are not going to die. And we have to hurry." I look to the dog. "We'll be back, boy. I promise."

James and I run up the stairs. I don't know what I think we're going to find: a battle underway, or frightened children. But this?

"Holy dragons," James says.

Facing the stairs, the chief stands still as a wax figurine. Blood runs down her cheeks. Her mouth is contorted, her teeth monstrous and vicious, and her hands raised, purple light halfway to its destination, frozen in midair.

It's headed straight for Smee's heart.

Wibbles and Damien Salt and Smee have weapons drawn and pointed at her. My friends. They tried to defend me after all. Exchanging a look, James and I work quickly to move the boys out of the way.

I could strangle the chief now, while she's vulnerable, or stab her like she did my family, but there's no honor in that. I want her in shackles. I want her brought to justice.

The Vanished are all over, scattered like toys on a bedroom floor. Some are crying. Some are crouched down, trying to take cover. Some bravely hold up their fists. These kids. We have to help them.

"Take cover!" James yells. "I can't hold it anymore!"

The chief's face twitches as she tries to move her fingers, like a doll coming to life.

"Ready or not, here we go!" I yell.

"Lost Boys!" he calls out. "It's time for mutiny!"

Mayhem starts up everywhere at once as James disappears.

"You're all going to walk the plank!" the chief screams, but no sooner has she spoken than Barnacle, wounded but still fighting, leaps from the stairwell onto the chief and knocks her down. Morgie swings around the corner. She flies past me and pulls Barnacle off the chief, flinging him to the side, just as Hellion swoops down.

"Get off me, you idiotic bird!" the chief screams, but Hellion only rears back and dives in again.

Barnacle gets back to his feet, looking confused. Morgie turns on me. "Why would you do this to us? We would have had everything."

The chief screams, unable to fend off Hellion's attack, her magic shooting in all directions but missing her mark. Light sparks at Morgie's fingertips. And they're aimed at me. She rears back, hissing like a snake, as Ursula swings around the corner on all her tentacles, sloshing, moving faster than I've ever seen her. "No, Morgie!" she yells, getting between Morgie and me. "Mary is our family."

"You're so weak," she says. "It makes me sick."

Ursula hurls light at Morgie's legs, which disappear, transforming into tentacles that match her sister's. Ursula picks up her sister and chucks her over the side of the ship as James reappears with irons in hand and wraps the chains around the chief in two quick movements, pinning her arms to her sides.

"Don't you move," Bella says, running up behind him. "Don't even try it."

The chief struggles to get free, screaming and straining, but nothing works.

Barnacle limps over, and Hellion flaps overhead.

A calm settles over the ship as the Vanished realize the chief can't hurt them. They find their friends, gather in small circles, comforting the younger among them.

"What now?" Lucas says, coming up behind me.

"I'll tell you what now," Ursula says. She leans over the chief and points. "You messed up, Chiefypoo. Our deal is off." She swishes over the side of the ship and raises both hands.

"You don't know what you're doing!" the chief says.

"I know *exactly* what I'm doing." Ursula sends purple light into the sea, which crackles with fingers of lightning long after Ursula is done, an underwater storm. The ship rocks, but the sky is placid above us.

"This is a mistake," the chief wails. "You don't understand!" For the first time since all this started, she looks terrified, eyes glued to the edge of the ship.

"I do understand. I understand exactly what's coming for you now," Ursula says.

A high-pitched cry interrupts the frenzy, and everyone stops what they're doing. It's Merryweather, hovering, wings flapping, wand in hand. Flora and Fauna flit out over the water.

"What is that?" Fauna says, clinging to Flora.

"It's bodies!" Flora yells, pointing downward. "It's bodies!"

"Darn right." Ursula grins. "Everybody gets their just desserts in the end."

"Urs," I say, "what did you do?"

"The chief didn't hold up her end of the bargain." Her eyes burn yellow as a grin slides over her face. "And you know I hate a welcher."

Her garden. All those people. She was holding them captive on behalf of the chief. And now she's set them free. But where were they before Ursula got to the bottom of the sea? How did the chief find them? I have so many questions, but they won't be answered now. There isn't time.

"No, Urs!" I yell over the mounting fray. "Where are they going to go? There's too many of them. They'll capsize us!"

Ursula shrugs. "I don't know what to tell you, sweetie. The deed is done."

Hands appear at the edge of the ships. They're wet, and fighting for purchase. For a moment I'm not sure if they're friends or foes, but when I see Mally's father, Jack Saint, pull himself to safety, I yell, "Help them! Now! Everyone!" Old people, young people, some I recognize and some I don't, pull themselves up over the edge. "Use your wands. Float them up!" The Vanished, who have been so well trained, rush to the side of the boats, and chant spells, pointing their wands at the water. A few of them use their wands to get people to safety.

Bella is frantically pulling people aboard, along with Lucas and the Lost Boys. Even Hat is helping now. I hear Bella cry out from the prow as she pulls Jasmine, sopping wet but breathing, into her arms. "You're going to be okay!"

A cracking noise splits the air. She has spoken too soon.

The ship begins to list, to tip.

The sea is brighter than before, filled with purple light.

"Mary," Bella yells as she pulls more people over. "The ships can't handle this. You have to take us home!"

For a second I'm not sure what she's saying. But then I realize . . . all this ends with me. I am the only one who can save us now. Fear cannot have me. All my inner chatter has to cease.

As survivors hang on to the ship, desperate to live, I think about the Scar. About home.

The lake flickers.

They scream and scream.

I feel like it will never be quiet again.

But the ships begin to rumble. The people climbing on board struggle and lose their balance. I strain to hold all the energy, all the lives, all the responsibility.

"Take us back to the Scar," I command from my gut. "Right now."

The sea goes from purple to swirling, bubbling red. It opens.

"Brace yourselves!" I warn. "Hold on for your lives!"

All of the ships fall through the water, through the portal I've made, into the world we come from, a roller coaster on its first descent. I prepare myself for pain, for death, for more and more and more loss.

But none of that happens.

Instead, it is calm—silent, even—as we land on top of Miracle Lake.

From here, I can see my apartment building, the city skyline, the warning signs all around the lake, the bobbing, floating street lights.

We've done it.

We're home.

I catch sight of the chief wriggling out of her chains. She chucks them to the side and runs straight for me, screaming, her face contorted. There are so many people on the deck of the ships, we're like fish in a net, squirming against each other. I only have a moment to absorb that with only a few exceptions, these people are wearing finery, the men in distressed tuxedos, the women in evening gowns and satin pants. The Vanished, discernible by their black clothes, are also running, trying to get to safety.

The chief grabs me by the throat, knocking me to the ground. In the chaos, I fear no one has even noticed. We are face-to-face, and I can't breathe.

"I should have finished you off with the rest of your family," she hisses in my ear. "I'll find a way to do what I want to do. I'm not going to let you or anyone else stop me." The world is wavering in and out of focus now, fading as she sits on my chest, presses into me, the cuts on her cheeks metallic-smelling. There's no Hellion to save me now, no sign of him anywhere. I hope he made it through the portal. I've lost track of Lucas and Bella, too.

This time she has me. Everyone is too busy saving themselves to come to my aid. I writhe, my body kicking furiously while I hover, no longer feeling any pain. This will be the end of my story.

It will not be happy or poetic or triumphant.

It will only be over.

BELLA

THE PORTAL KNOCKS BELLA DOWN. IT WRECKS her, flattens her like she's being crushed by the weight of the ships and all the people on it. She struggles for breath. The last thing she saw before the portal opened was the chief wriggling free of the irons. She knows disaster is imminent, that Charlene Ito won't go down easy.

Her ears are ringing, the sounds of shouting and crying all around her. She can't see.

She's sweating, shivering. Finally, she can feel herself breathing again. She scrambles on all fours, pushing bodies off her.

There is water everywhere, detritus sloshing here and there. Teacups, saucers, ropes. The pool on the main deck has emptied out, and people are slipping into it. All these people. Bella doesn't know how they got here, but she has stared at the pictures of the victims of the Fall for long enough to know who they are. Thousands of people, presumed dead, risen up.

Great ghost, she thinks.

She has to find Mary.

She scans the deck and spots the chief, in her white suit, out in the sea of black.

Sirens begin to wail all around them. It sounds like angels weeping.

A chopper clicks overhead.

Maybe help is on the way.

Bella looks again. The chief is bent over, on her knees like so many of the rest of them, but there is something under her. Bella sees kicking legs. She knows those boots. Her mind is working, making connections, losing its dizziness, shucking its fog.

That's Mary Elizabeth. The chief is on her.

Bella feels a burst of strength and clambers to her feet. From her left, she feels more than sees Ursula using her tentacles to climb over the sandpile of the suffering.

"Hey! Hey you!" Bella turns and see that Ursula has something in her hand. It is a glass container filled with golden liquid.

Bella does not like Ursula.

Ursula is not a good person.

But she thinks Ursula loves Mary, and right now that is enough for her.

Ursula and Bella can't reach each other. They make eye contact. Bella communicates with Ursula, assures her she will catch it. Bella used to play softball. She was very good at it. She knows she can do this.

Ursula hurls the ampoule at Bella.

Bella pretends it's a baseball. She pretends it's the game of the year. She can't let the stakes sink in. She has to keep her head in this moment and this moment only.

The glass pirouettes in midair. The golden liquid sloshes. It is beautiful.

She catches it.

CITY OF MAGIC AND MONSTERS

Ursula slips from view.

She runs, hard, stepping on people, kicking hands from her ankles.

If she can get this shining liquid to Mary, everything will be okay.

She doesn't know how she knows this, but she does.

She feels it.

Her Seed mark is glowing.

Bella's magic is alive.

SIXTEEN

Portalers know and understand this truth:
Magic cannot go anywhere. It is the infinite intelligence.
It is always with us. We think the trick to closing portals is
to work with magic and to give it what it wants.

—*A People's History of the Scar*

ONE SECOND, THE CHIEF IS ON ME, AND THE NEXT she is yanked back by an unseen force.

"I'll kill you," she spits, over and over again, like she can't say it enough times. "I'll kill you I'll kill you I'll kill you." Even as she loses her grip on my throat, she whispers the words, and I feel her willing them to be true.

Bella is here.

She pulls me up. My vision is still spotty, but relief rushes through me as my breath returns. I struggle as my airways open, my body flooded with adrenaline. While I'm still getting my bearings, Bella opens my palm and puts something cold and wet into it. She folds my fingers over it.

CITY OF MAGIC AND MONSTERS

I look down. It's the antidote. I don't know how she got it or where it came from, but I recognize the liquid.

The chief knocks Bella to the side. Bella hits the boards with a solid smack.

That's enough from the chief.

It's enough.

I uncork the bottle.

The chief opens her mouth to say something. Probably to threaten me again. She never gets the chance. I attack with the full force of my anger, pin her down with red electricity as she writhes. I pour the liquid over her lips.

I don't know what will happen next. Maybe nothing.

But then the chief begins to shrivel. Her skin sinks. Her nose grows. Her hair turns white. Her teeth rot.

I lean down. Even with the noise all around us, I'm sure she can hear me. "That's for my family, you monster." The chief reaches for me and I crawl backward away from her. Ursula suctions her way toward us, nailing the chief with a new flash of light. Ito shrinks, the sharp curves of her body losing their definition. Within seconds, she's a wriggling worm with eyes, soft-bellied and helpless.

"Don't you mess with Mary," Ursula says, scooping her up into her palm. "I know just the place for you."

I don't have time to feel the victory as I push up to my feet. I've got to help all these people. I rush for the side of the ship as a new commotion starts up.

The water roils, bubbling and folding in on itself.

"What is this?" Bella asks.

"I don't know," I say. "Everyone back!"

As the people around me try to follow instructions, clustering on the deck, something rises from the water.

"Horns," I whisper.

"Well, will you look at that," Ursula murmurs.

Bella gives me a worried look. "What is she talking about?"

But before I have the chance to answer, Mally rises from the water like she's riding an invisible elevator, and she has someone in her arms, a woman with long black hair. Mally's purple eyes survey us all as she floats up and, without a word, settles aboard the ship. She drops to her knees, placing the woman safely in a corner. I recognize her from the vision in the staff. It's Mally's mother.

James runs to her and as she looks up at him, she smiles the smile of someone who has walked a hundred miles and finally reached her destination. Even with all the chaos on the ship, her relief touches me.

All around me, people are using the lifeboats from the ships to get to the edge of Miracle as firefighters offer helping hands and extend boards to help. A crowd is forming, people coming from every side of the lake.

The Vanished are going back to their families. Flora and Fauna fly into their parents' arms, as I watch Smee and James and the Lost Boys guiding the children home.

And the people who were in the Wand . . . they're finding their loved ones, too. Cries of fear have turned joyful. Hope is all around me.

So many wishes come true.

A peace descends over me in the midst of the wildness on deck.

Mally has her family back. All the children will be home tonight.

A small piece of the wound I carry heals.

This is over. It really is.

CITY OF MAGIC AND MONSTERS

"Mary! Mary! Mary!" Aunt Gia sprints across a wobbly bridge, clambering aboard, moving against the stream. It's the first time I've seen her outside our apartment in ten years. She wraps me up in her arms and the smells of sugared citrus. I hug her and hold her. "I'm so sorry, Auntie G," I say. "For everything I've put you through. It wasn't fair."

"That's okay, my love," she croons. "Nothing ever is."

But it's not okay.

The earth begins to shake, a little at first, then more intensely. Cries go up all around me.

"James!" I yell, letting go of Gia as I search for him.

But my voice drowns in the void as thousands of crows fall out of the storm clouds, cawing and circling above in a tornado of feathers. A flock of flamingoes tear down Desire Avenue, toward the lake. Eels slither from the gutters, and people scream and try to get away. But they only find themselves running into hedgehogs, which are rolling down the city streets. Sirens blare everywhere as the earth shakes again.

"I'm here, Mare," James says.

Across from us, Mally separates from her parents and joins us. The Lost Boys run over, too, and Ursula finds her way to us.

"What the hell is going on?" Smee says. "This is not cool at all."

"There's going to be another Fall!" a woman shouts, clutching her drenched pashmina around her pale, bare shoulders. "Look!"

Blue light is brewing in the water, slipping and swishing, flashing so brightly we have to shield our eyes.

"What is this?" I shout.

"Looks like magic's not done yet," Mally says.

"We have to get everyone off the ship!" James yells. "Now!"

It's chaos. People are going to get hurt. They're going to die.

202

Now is not the time to panic. *Think, Mary, think.*

The book.

It said the only way to save everyone and everything is to close any portals that have been opened. How am I going to do that? I've been portaling all over the place like it's nothing, so proud of myself for my accomplishments.

But maybe . . . What if . . .

"We have to sacrifice ourselves," I say to my friends. "Magic is a living, breathing thing, right? So let's give ourselves to it." I turn to the lake. "Come on!" James looks to Mally, and Mally looks to Ursula. An understanding passes between us. And the earth gives another snakelike shake.

The ground begins to split under our feet, and I think this time the whole Scar will disappear, not just the ground we're standing on.

"Hey!" I yell. "Magic. Great ghost."

The rumbling settles. The light swirls and swishes beneath the water's surface.

"Will you take us?" I say.

The water bubbles like a giant has emptied its lungs.

"Take us, and leave the Scar alone," I say. "Please."

Everything is silent. No sirens. No one wailing. Everyone is watching. I feel all of Monarch beside me, all the people who are probably watching this live from all over the globe. I feel the whole world at my back.

The crows overhead squawk. The ground shakes. Blue light rises out of the lake, and I squeeze my eyes shut so I don't get blinded.

I hold on to James, ready for the end.

But the end doesn't come.

The hedgehogs disappear.

The crows retreat.

CITY OF MAGIC AND MONSTERS

The flamingoes stand around the lake.

Hovering in front of us, in midair, three perfect portals appear.

They are oval in shape, like windows into storybooks. One is hilly, with a castle visible in the distance. One is green, with perfect hedges, and filled with roses, and the last is the rolling ocean and majestic ships of Neverland.

I heave a sigh and slump over, my knees nearly giving out. I look from side to side at my friends, see their resignation, and understand. This is really happening. We really don't get to stay in the Scar. We're never going back to high school, and we'll never be able to live in Monarch again.

"Say your goodbyes," Mally says.

"Aw, Mal," James says. "You just got your family back."

"Oh, don't worry," she says. "They're coming with me. They just don't know it yet."

My James is here with me now.

His fire is gone, he looks less feverish, and the flush that was raging against his skin has settled. "This is over, isn't it?" he says. "You and me?"

"You want to live on a boat," I say. "You want to be a pirate. Magic is giving you Neverland. You have to go."

"And you?" he asks. "What do you want?"

I think of my room on the ship, the roses. "I want to be myself, and make my own rules. I want to live in a world where my family could be dead, but also alive, because reality means nothing there. I want strange adventures and joy and wonder. I want flowers everywhere. But mostly, I don't want anyone to tell me what to do anymore."

James considers me for a long moment, the air grown heavy enough to feel like fingers digging into my lungs. Then he says, "That sounds nice."

We sit there in silence awhile.

I let it all sink in. Sometimes when you say the worst things out loud, you realize even it won't kill you. At least, the words won't all by themselves.

Then all you can do is live with it.

"You need someone who wants to travel the high seas with you," I say, gently. "That's never going to be me. I need my feet on the ground and my head in the clouds." I lean my head against his shoulder one last time. "You'll always be my pirate boy," I say.

He smiles a sad smile. "Mare, I'm not ever going to know another girl like you. You'll always be my queen." He stands and pulls me to my feet. Barnacle trots over to him, sensing it's time to go. "Let's do this," he says. "Let's write the end of this story."

"And the beginning of the next one."

"I love you, Mare," he says, pulling me in to hug me. "I always will. You know that, right?"

"I love you, too." I tug his hook. "Hey," I say, "don't die, okay?"

"Ah," he says, "we can't die. The world would be way too boring without us."

Tears threaten.

"It's going to be okay," he says. "Promise. And if anyone messes with you, just remember . . ."

"Remember what?"

"Fists up, Mare." He smiles again. It's almost enough to hide the sadness lingering there.

CITY OF MAGIC AND MONSTERS

"Fists up," I say.

We have spent all our lives fighting in one way or another, mostly together. But I'm ready to stand on my own.

First responders are all around us. The lake has been emptied. Only the boats sit on the water.

I take one last look around at my beautiful city and at my friends. Ursula, James, Smee, and all the boys are going back to Neverland. I am going somewhere else, to the green place. Mally is going to the castle. Of course she is.

We hug each other, one by one.

"I'm going to miss you, toots," Urs says.

"You have been the best friend. The very best," I say.

"I know." She winks at me and dives through, back into Neverland and down into the depths of the ocean with all those mermaids and strange creatures and her skeleton house. I think she'll be happier there than she would have been back in the Scar. At least I hope so.

"Mare." James puts a gentle hand on my shoulder. "She's going to be okay. I'll be there to look out for her if she needs me."

"I know that," I say with a sniffle. "I'm not worried about her."

"But saying goodbye hurts, doesn't it?" James lifts my chin and gazes deeply into my eyes before resting his hook on my shoulder. It does hurt, to know this will likely be the last time I see him. I don't know how I'll get by without my friend, without any of my friends. They've been everything to me, always. "You sure you're good with this plan?" he asks.

"I am." I don't know how to tell him that the distress of leaving the Scar behind feels like a season being swept away in a pile of leaves, leaving bare branches, clear skies, and all the potential of everything that's to come. It's scary, but I'm looking forward to it, and I hope that when I step through the portal, I will find a new, brighter, happier me on the other side.

I take his hook off my shoulder and get on my tiptoes to kiss his cheek. "Go get your ship, Cap!"

"Yeah?" he says, sparkling as he eyes the ship.

"Hop on board," I say, as James and Barnacle cross the bridge, followed closely by a train of Lost Boys. "But promise me you're going to give her a new name, a fresh start for a new adventure."

"Like what?"

"How about the *Jolly Roger*?" Smee suggests. "You know . . . after my first cat."

"That sounds great," James says, clapping Smee on his back. "It's the perfect name."

Smee's cheeks pink as I crouch down and bury my nose in Barnacle's fur. "Goodbye. Take care of James and the boys for me."

He lays a paw on my knee and bends to touch his forehead to mine.

When James, Barnacle, and the boys are all huddled I say, "Ready?"

"Ready for adventure, always!" James says, already turning away from me, to his future. "We have a whole world to discover."

While they're all chattering excitedly about all the things they're going to see, I use the drawbridge to get back to the side of the lake. I spin my hand and the circle widens to accept them. I send the whole boat through the portal, and when it closes, it leaves only the *Legacy* and the *Loyalty* behind, bobbing on the water, empty.

"I think it's my turn," Mally says, Hellion standing so regally on her shoulder.

I reach up to stroke his feathers. He is soft and silky. "A day of goodbyes," I say.

"But also hellos," she says as her parents come to stand at her side, holding hands.

"What are you going to do?" I ask Jack Saint. "What about being the mayor and everything? What about all your property, everything you wanted? Are you sure you want to go?"

"You know," he says, standing to his full height as he surveys the cityscape, "I got so ambitious, I forgot what was important to me. I got greedy." He looks around at the Scar. "It's time, I think, to leave all this behind. To be free. To find something new."

"I want to thank you for everything you did," Mally says. "For hearing me in your dreams, for taking care of Hellion, for making sure I came back."

"I didn't do all that alone."

"Still," she says.

"I'm happy for you. And I'm so glad you came back."

"I'm happy for you, too," she says. "I have a feeling we're going to do great things."

"I hope so," I say. "I really do."

As gently as possible, I shepherd Mally and her family through the portal. Mally's mother and Jack look back from the patch of grass they're standing on, and in the distance I see a huge castle, pink and blue flags flying in the distance. Mally, her black collar reaching up high, her staff firmly planted in the ground, nods at me. It's her face I see, as I close the portal.

It's my turn now. This is going to be harder than I thought. I love the Scar. I love Gia and Bella and maybe even Lucas a little bit, too. And this is such a special place. Maybe it won't have magic after all, but that doesn't mean it isn't magical.

Gia and Bella, who have been watching from a distance, come over to me, along with Lucas and Hat.

"You sure you don't want me to come with you?" Gia asks.

I squeeze her hand. "No. I think I've got to do this alone. And besides, you need to sell the apartment, go live on the beach like you always wanted. It's going to be great."

She cups my cheek. "I love you, Mary Elizabeth. And I'm proud of you." And then we're hugging each other for so long, the portal zaps its blue light at me.

Magic is growing impatient.

I hug Lucas next. "Thanks for everything," I say. "You're all right, you know that?"

"You're okay yourself. And hey, maybe I can come visit you someday."

"Yeah," I say. "If I can figure out how to get you there without tearing the world apart."

"I bet you will," he says. "I'd bet money you'll do just that." He gives me a half smile. "Stay humble, Mary."

"Oh, Lucas," I say, giving his hand a squeeze. "I don't aspire to being humble. I aspire to have a great adventure."

"I'm sure you're going to do that."

"And hey . . ."

"Yeah?"

"So you know, whatever debt you thought you owed because of your dad? The slate is clean, okay? I know when you get your inheritance, you're going to do great things with it." I tap his chest, and we look into each other's eyes. There's so much in there, so much fire. Lucas is going to be okay.

"Thanks, Mary," he says.

Finally, I get to Bella. I can't look at her. If I do, I might never leave, and magic most certainly wouldn't stand for that. "You take care of the Scar, okay?"

She wipes at her cheek. "I promise."

I take one last look around the Scar, my sad and amazing home. I am going to miss it so much.

"Goodbye," I say, steeling myself against a wave of emotion. "I'll be just on the other side of everywhere." Before I can hesitate, I fling myself through the portal. But instead of just taking me, the blue light extends itself outward, wrapping Hat in its hands and yanking him through with me. I search for him, in a panic, but he's nowhere I can see.

The trip seems longer this time than ever before, like I'm falling down a long tube. As I go, a ticking clock floats by me, a nightstand with a vase of flowers on top, an upside-down umbrella. It's as though the whole world has come unscrewed and is reordering itself.

With a thump, I land on a bed of roses, rich and red, and soft as velvet.

I sit up, and find myself surrounded by green pastures. I can breathe the air. I hear birds squawking and, in the distance, singing.

"Hello," a voice drawls.

In front of me, a disembodied smile appears.

I'm not afraid.

A crown thuds to the ground next to me. It's red and sharp and decorated with ruby hearts. I pick it up. "Thank you, magic," I whisper, and place it on my head.

Yes.

I can make this place a home.

BELLA

TWO YEARS LATER . . .

BELLA LOYOLA SITS AT HER DESK IN THE Monarch City Police Department. She is the youngest police chief in the history of the city, and she still loves her nameplate. She swipes it with a yellow cloth, removing all traces of dust, as the screens on her wall play out the news of the day.

A muralist has made a new piece in the center of the Scar, of the once-villains, now-heroes, those willing to sacrifice themselves for the good of many. The unveiling is the biggest news since the second Battle of Miracle Lake, but Bella will continue to be here . . . just in case. She was right, it seems, that magic was too dangerous for Monarch. It is better now that it is gone, in the hands of few rather than at the whim of many.

No matter. She's got speeches to give, precincts to visit, and commendations to deliver. That horrible partner of hers from before

CITY OF MAGIC AND MONSTERS

Mary . . . Tony . . . she finally has him dead to rights for harassment, and she can't wait to meet with him later.

Bella's intercom beeps. She pulls her attention away from the screen and pushes a button. "Yes?"

"Jasmine Bizhan is on line two for you," her new assistant, Cybil, says. "You said always to put her through."

"Yes," she says. "Thank you."

Jasmine is laughing when Bella presses the button for line two. "Wow, that Cybil couldn't be more starstruck, eh?"

"Oh," Bella says. "It'll burn off."

"I don't know . . . I think she might be a real fan."

"And you . . ." Bella says, changing the subject. "How are you?"

"I never thought I'd say this, but I kind of wish something would happen, something exciting or even scary. Everyone is behaving themselves so well, life is getting a little dull." Her voice muffles. Bella can hear Abu chittering in the background, and Al asking Jasmine what she wants for dinner. Jasmine's voice comes clear again as Bella spins in her chair so she can peruse the pictures on her office wall. Maleficent flying over the city in dragon form, Ursula ten stories high, and finally Bella and Mary, arms slung around each other's shoulders, grinning broadly in the days before Mary was taken over by the Red Queen, before she started wrestling beasts Bella couldn't help her with.

"Yeah," Bella says, her throat constricting, "I miss the good old days sometimes myself. But in the end, we're better off now."

"It was nice of Mary and the others to do what they did."

Bella feels sick for a moment. Occasionally, she misses Mary so much she can't breathe. She even almost misses her brief moment of being magical. But at least Mary and Hat have each other. And they have magic, too. The right kind. She can take comfort in that. "You be safe," she says.

"Yeah," Jasmine says. "Let's get together soon."

"Brunch for sure." Bella spins around in her chair, and gasps.

There on her desk is a small white box with a red ribbon around it. She looks at the box for a moment, then presses the intercom button. "Cybil, did you come in here just now?" Bella is quite sure she didn't have her back turned for more than a minute, but the mind can play tricks sometimes.

"What? No!" Cybil stammers. "I've been out here the whole time. I mean . . . Okay, I did get a little distracted for a second, but—"

"Okay, got it, thanks," Bella says, and clicks off. She reminds herself to be patient. She was eager once. Cybil will calm down. And this is how people look at her now. This is how they treat her. Like she's someone important and powerful.

Because she is.

She returns to the box, heart hammering. Her Seed mark buzzes, a sensation she hasn't felt since . . . well, since Mary left. This box is sparking with magic.

Lucas must have succeeded. Ever since he got his money, he's been working on a safe way to move through worlds, he and that white rabbit he retrieved from Dally Star's after Mary left. That means . . . maybe he found Mary. Maybe Mary can leave that place now. Maybe . . .

Lucas is hard to reach these days, but he would take her call. She will find out what he's up to.

Bella's mind is spinning.

EAT ME, the tag says.

She hopes.

For what, she isn't sure.

Not yet.

Tentatively, Bella pulls the red ribbon off and slides it to the side, where it lands in a pile of curlicues. She opens the box like it might have a grenade inside. One never knows . . . even with Monarch as quiet as it is these days, anything could happen.

Inside, the box is lined in red satin, and sitting on it is a single rectangle of the most beautiful heart-shaped confection she has ever seen. She lifts it to her lips and takes a bite, and a song starts up. She is certain it is for her ears only, that the tinkling wisp of music is a gift along with the melting sugar on her tongue. She is certain, too, that this tiny taste of magic is a sign to her that Mary is alive and well.

Somewhere, she is causing mischief, making magic, and filling her world with wonder.

ACKNOWLEDGMENTS

TATTOO HEARTS AND LEATHER JACKETS TO YOU, Jocelyn Davies. I have treasured our collaboration and loved building this world with you. Thank you for being such a lovely editor and person. Many thanks also to Cassandra Phan and Kieran Viola for your invaluable editorial contributions. Phil Buchanan and Marci Senders, thank you for the epic design; to Augusta Harris for book-to-film and content packaging. Great Ghost, thanks, and thanks again to Sara Liebling, Guy Cunningham, Karen Krumpak, and Dan Kaufman for the Managing Editorial/Copyediting; to Vicki Korlishin and Monique Diman for all your work in sales. Much gratitude to Matt Schweitzer, Holly Nagel, Danielle DiMartino, and Dina Sherman for your efforts in marketing; and of course to Crystal McCoy, Daniela Escobar, and Kelly Forsythe in PR. The teamwork and creativity at Disney is its own miracle, one I will not forget.

To Emily van Beek, my perfect agent and friend, I love you always. Thank you for everything, forever.

And thank you to my family, my friends, my students, my colleagues, and my spectacular husband and children. I wouldn't *be* without you.

Finally, thank you to all the readers for sticking with me through thick and thin. Pixie dust and magic wands to all of you!